Venom and Vows

A romantic regency-inspired fantasy
Written by
MAEGWEN SALLEY-MASSIE

An imprint of Green Ferns Publishing House
Copyright © 2025 Green Ferns Publishing House. Cover designed by Candice Yamnitz. Interior designed by Nora Smith.

Library of Congress Cataloging-in-Publication Data
Salley-Massie, Maegwen
Venom and vows/ Maegwen Salley-Massie
185 pages.

Summary: "A young girl must face an arranged marriage while also competing for a vampire's sponsorship, yet she plans to race in a forbidden horse race—all to pay her family's debt and free herself, but everything goes wrong." -provided by publisher

ISBN 979-8-9996047-2-9
Subjects: Fantasy—Fiction. Romance—Fiction. Regency—Fiction.

Printed in the United States of America

Contents

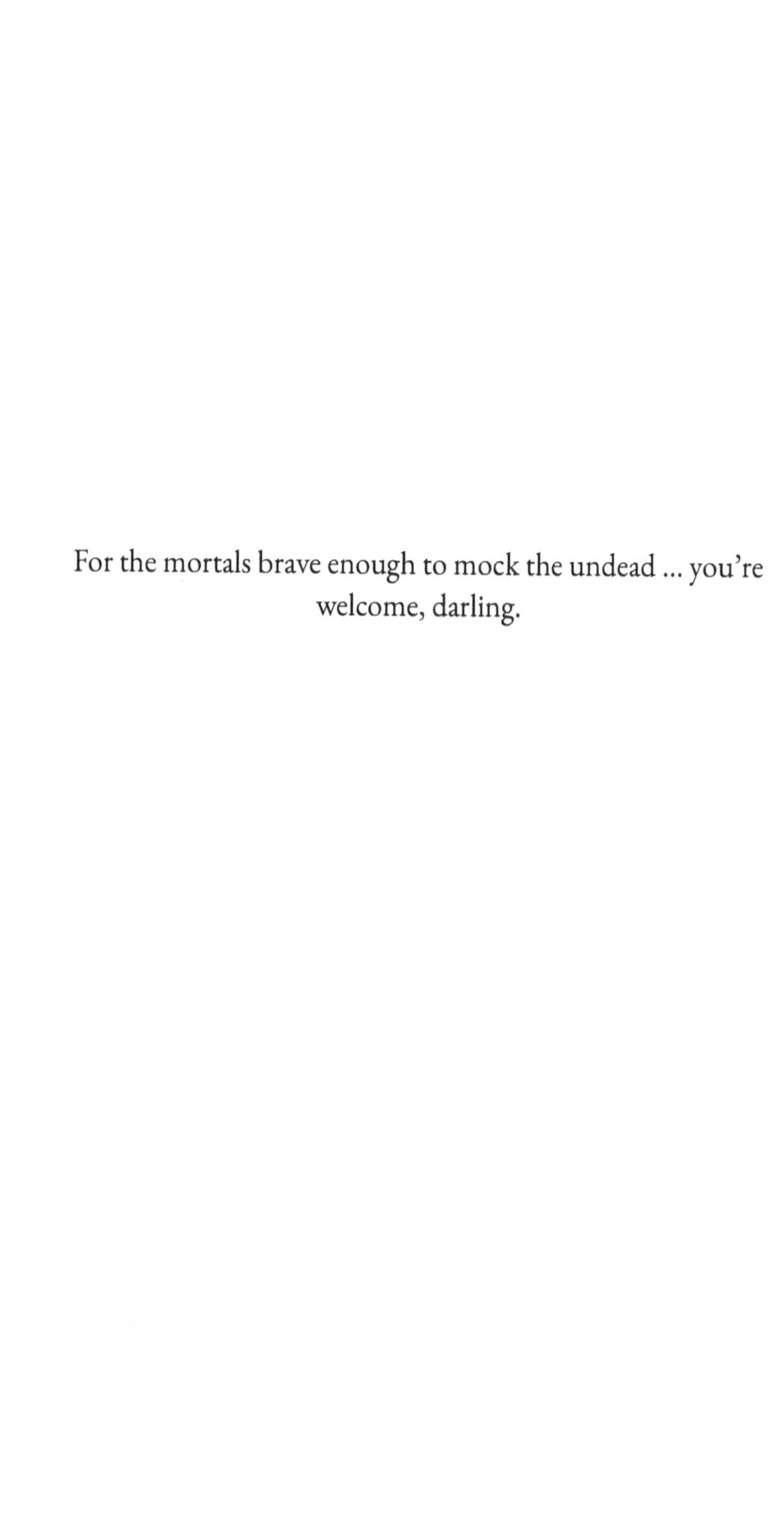

For the mortals brave enough to mock the undead … you're welcome, darling.

Thornveil Isle

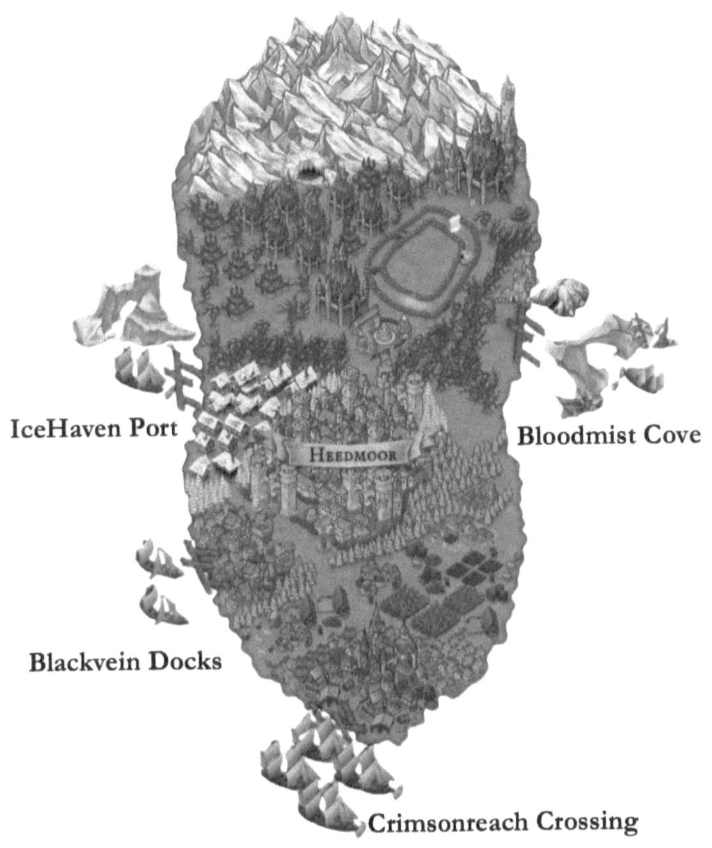

Congratulations,
You are cordially invited to attend

Venom
and
Vows

This year's five-night affair promises to eclipse all those before it. Pray, come well-prepared, and do not fail to delight your most discerning hosts—the Vampires of Thornveil Isle.

CHAPTER ONE

The Injury

A loud scream rang out across the frosted spinach gardens, causing Seraphina to drop her basket. *No. No. No. Please, no!* The sound was filled with pain and tears. She hiked up her skirts and started running through the dirt and snow, dread weighing down every step. She had warned him—no, commanded him—not to touch the axe. She made him swear that only Father could use that sharp tool.

She skidded around the crumbling stone fencing, catching herself on the broken horse statue. Its left ear was missing, lost long ago, and it had gained several more cracks and chips. Her eyes fixed on the crying young boy of only seven, wailing in the arms of her eldest brother, Simon; then she saw the blood.

Crimson flowed from the axe, which was still embedded in her youngest brother's leg, staining the white snow. Shiloh screamed out as his father yanked the tool from his flesh. More dark blood pooled from the open gash. Seraphina grabbed her aching chest and ran to the circle of chaos.

"What can I do? What can I do?" she asked breathlessly, words coming out in clouds, pale and fleeting.

"Go grab alcohol and more cloths!" her father said loudly, full of panic and worry.

She didn't have to, though. Shiloh's twin sister was already running to the bloody scene with large tears rolling down her pale, rosy cheeks.

Father grabbed the alcohol. "Well done, Sophia. Now, hurry back to the house. This is no place for you. Your brothers and I will handle this."

"But ..." she whimpered.

"Now, Sophia!"

The dark-haired child jumped and scampered back to the house.

Shiloh writhed against his brothers' grip, unable to free himself as he lay on the snowy ground. Seraphina's father held his uninjured leg, while Simon and Seymour detained his arms and upper body. Simon and Seymour, the second-born, looked clearly alike, sharing their father's dark curly hair and brown eyes, yet Seymour was born with a disproportionate right side. Everything on his right side was smaller than his left: ear, eye, arm, and hand. Even his leg was shorter, causing him to walk with a slight limp.

Seraphina knew her role. She would be the one to administer the alcohol, stitch the wound, and wrap it. Holding her breath, she popped the cork and poured the contents onto the wound. Shiloh screeched, then thankfully passed out. She worked quickly, cleaning and stitching as fast and efficiently as possible. Once she finished wrapping his leg, Simon scooped Shiloh into his arms and carried him into the cottage, leaving the dirt soaked in blood.

Seraphina looked at her father's blood-stained hands, a testament to how close they had come to losing another family member. The pain of her mother's death overwhelmed her, making her feel dizzy. Nausea hit her like a strong gust of wind; she turned and vomited.

She heard her brother's hobbling footsteps on the snow as he approached her and saw his outstretched hand, holding a small handkerchief.

"Easy, sister. Everything's fine."

Seraphina snatched the handkerchief. "Fine?" she said incredulously, wiping her mouth. "How did your brain calculate that everything is fine? Did you take into consideration that our youngest brother almost sliced through his leg? He could have lost it and become a cripple, or he could have bled out and died."

With his always stern, emotionless exterior, Seymour nodded once and replied, "But he didn't, and now, he will be *fine*." He spun on his heels and walked toward their home.

"That's it?"

"Seraphina ..." Her father called to her with his scolding tone that added a hint of don't-press-your brother mixed with a dash of you-know-how-he-is.

She hated how unattached to human emotion Seymour was; sometimes, he seemed like he wasn't human at all. Seraphina had even slipped into his bedroom just to check his pulse—she had to know. She wouldn't sleep under the same roof as a ...

"Seraphina, you know better than to argue with Seymour." Her father repeatedly pushed and pulled the icy well pump handle, then started washing his hands once the chilling water came out. "Shiloh was lucky. He wasn't strong enough to swing the axe with much force. That's what saved his life and leg."

Seraphina folded the handkerchief and slipped it into the side pocket of her apron; this one she wouldn't give back to her brother. She wrapped her arms around herself, hoping the cold would leave her in peace for just a moment.

"The doctor should come check on him."

Her father grabbed a rag, drying his hands. "You know we can't afford that." He tossed the damp cloth onto the pile of uncut wood covered in layers of snow, daring his daughter to contest him. "I'll have Ms. Hatley come by to help. He'll need someone to watch over him and your sister anyway for tonight."

Tonight. Tonight would be a complete disaster. Amid all the chaos this morning, she had forgotten about tonight. She wished her leg was wounded; that way, she wouldn't have to go. Seraphina nodded, hoping that would satisfy her father. "Are you looking forward to it and the festivities?" her father asked with wishful eyes.

Seraphina tilted her head, anger boiling inside. "Why yes, Father. I'm excited to be paraded around a room full of blood-thirsty creatures and auctioned off to a cold-hearted vampire—that's even if one would deem me worthy of his attention."

CHAPTER TWO

Halloways

Seraphina Halloway loathed this season. Everyone who could pay the entry fee applied for an invitation to Venom and Vows, the year's debutante contest. Most kingdoms preferred having boys, but here in Heedmoor, parents desired daughters, not because daughters are better than sons or vice versa, but because daughters offer the chance to secure luxury beyond a family's wildest dreams. If a family has a daughter, parents spend the year saving enough money for lessons in the art of becoming the perfect lady, all to get their greedy hands on vampire venom—the most expensive and valuable substance in all the lands.

For the past several years, Seraphina hadn't attended the celebrations because of her mother's illness. Her father invested nearly all his earnings in trying to find a cure, using potions, spells, and medicines, but nothing worked. In the end, no amount of wealth could save her mother, especially when death is the ultimate decision maker.

Seraphina felt her anxiety melt away as she entered the stables. She inhaled the familiar smell of hay and the earthy scent of their horses. She untied her pale linen apron, stained with her brother's blood and dark soil, and hung it on her usual hook beside Velamir's stall.

She threw her arms around her shining white horse, Velamir; he would be her family's saving grace. But he wasn't an ordinary horse. No, Velamir had a secret, one Seraphina had to take to her grave. One immersed in the mysterious charm of unicorns and the quiet courage of legendary thoroughbreds. He was a creature like no other.

Seraphina dug into a pocket of her short, faded indigo gown and pulled out a crumpled piece of paper, the invitation to Venom and Vows. She huffed, wishing the exasperation could defile the snobs. Once a year, in the enchanting land of Heedmoor, vampires bind themselves to human families, supplying vampire venom, the elixir of immortality, to their chosen lineage in exchange for the lifeblood of humanity. Vampires select the daughters they will sponsor for the upcoming year at the legendary grand ball, after the ladies go through numerous days of parading in front of the vile bloodsucking creatures.

Seraphina flipped the invitation to look at the back. It told of a horse race, but to her, it symbolized freedom. To celebrate the end of Venom and Vows, noblemen competed in a challenging and daring horse race through miles of obstacles, stirring anticipation and suspense among all who watched. This horse race, however, had prize winnings that could pay off Seraphina's family's debts, saving them from financial ruin.

Neither of her older brothers were good at horse racing. Simon focused on farming and woodworking, while Seymour enjoyed his books and figures. Sure, if Seraphina had taken lessons for years, she might have a chance of landing a vamp, but she wasn't stupid and didn't live in a fantasy world. Seraphina Halloway was as far from the perfect lady as the sun is from the moon. She knew it. Her family knew it, and everyone in the village knew it, too.

Her father had insisted that he spend his last coins on the entry fee for Venom and Vows. What a waste. He could have bought a goat, which, now that she thought about it, the goat probably stood a better chance at wooing a vamp than she did. She laughed and straightened Velamir's head covering. She marveled at his icy blue eyes, loving that they matched hers and his secret.

"I think we need to stretch those mighty legs of yours. What do you think? Care for a run?"

Seraphina jumped at the sound of a man's voice behind her, quickly sliding the invitation back in her pocket.

"Miss Halloway, are we speaking to horses now?"

With slow movements, her woolen petticoat, the color of oatmeal, brushed against her dirty boots, its hem stiff with cold, reminding her of just how uncomfortable she was. Seraphina turned to face the figure. Her insides churned like spoiled milk on a hot summer day.

"Ah, Lord Beaumont, good day to you." She gave a small curtsey, irritated that this bug was stealing her riding time.

Lord Beaumont waved his white-gloved hand. "Oh, please, do call me Jared. I think we can forego the formalities."

Seraphina hesitated. *What did he mean by this?* Surely, he didn't mean ... "Forego? Forgive me, my lord, but I'm not sure I understand."

Jared folded his arms behind his back and took a daring step forward, causing Seraphina to press her back against the horse stall door. Jared Beaumont was a man accustomed to getting what he wanted; his looks and wealth supported that. He was a marquess with an estate as large as his ego. Seraphina could smell cedarwood and vanilla wafting from him, as if he were trying to enchant her.

He wore a stylish three-piece suit, the color of a stormy sea, and slicked back his chocolate brown hair. Jared smiled, his bright teeth standing out against his freshly trimmed beard. He always kept his beard full but thin, never thick.

"I'm so glad you asked, sweetheart." He pulled a red rose from behind his back and presented it to her. "I've just finished having a stirring conversation with your father."

Seraphina nearly gagged at the pet name, sweetheart. "My father?"

Jared raised an eyebrow and dangled the rose back and forth, annoying Seraphina enough that she took it. He grabbed her other hand and pressed it to his chest. "He's given his permission for me to marry you."

With the softest sound, the rose hit the ground; petals dusted with stable life. Seraphina's mouth fell open. She was speechless. What could she say? What could she do? She didn't love this man, nor did he love her. She understood why he wanted her. She wasn't in a position to gain wealth by earning vampire favor, nor had she received any prominent marriage proposals. He wanted her because she would owe him—she prayed he would forget he ever knew her.

She fought back tears. This wasn't the life she wanted. She wished her mother were here to fight for her, to be a shoulder to cry on, to kiss her brow and tell her everything would be okay. But this marriage proposal was anything but that.

His body closed the distance between them, and she felt his lips on her fingers as he kissed them. They were warm and felt like chains locking around her wrists.

He looked up into her eyes. "Miss Seraphina Halloway, you'll make a stunning wife."

CHAPTER THREE

The Realization

Tears streamed down Seraphina's cheeks as she rode Velamir, his hooves plowing into the snow. Engaged. How could she be engaged? Jared Beaumont was known to entertain several women of questionable reputations. Why would he be the chosen one? This couldn't be her life; she kept trying to wake up. Wake up from this terrible nightmare. The nightmare where her mother was dead, her family was bankrupt—on the verge of homelessness, her little brother nearly didn't make it, and she had to be in a loveless marriage, promised to owe her husband forever.

They stopped at the desolate ruins of the ancient guest house. It had fallen apart centuries ago, leaving only a ghostly gray stone frame that remained mostly intact. Layers of ice coated the stones, a somber reminder of the past memories once shared between the walls. She dismounted and walked inside to her secret hiding spot, leaving small footprints in the snow. Wiping her nose, she wiggled several large floor stones free to reveal her stash of men's clothing.

The hidden compartment smelled damp, like mildew, but she didn't mind. She had taken old, worn-out clothes from her eldest brother years ago and kept adding to her stash as she grew. Seraphina braided her hair quickly, strands clinging to her tears. She removed her dress and undergarments, then slipped into brown trousers and a stained shirt. She stuffed her feet into oversized, worn boots, wrapped her head and face with a long scarf, topped it with a ripped hat, and finished by looping her arms through a gentleman's coat.

She had to pass as a man; she needed to. Now, more than ever, she must win the horse race. The prize money would mean she wouldn't have to marry Lord Jared; if she lost, well, she'd be no better off. However, if she were caught racing, she'd be killed—after all, the penalty for women participating in the horse race was death. Her hands went to her neck, thinking she could be either beheaded or hanged. She wasn't sure which choice was the better one. Was there a better one between the two?

She sighed as she petted the geminox's nose, the proper term for his kind since he was a mix between a unicorn and a horse. His nostrils flared with boredom. He was ready to run; so was she, but for very different reasons. How had her life come to this? To have a life was to either parade herself before vamps or marry someone who was a complete rake. No. She realized she would rather face death than be trapped for the rest of her life. But what about her family?

She stepped back from the shimmering white creature and let out a loud grunt of frustration. "What am I to do?" She half wished her dear secret pet would answer her, a faint thought, though she knew it couldn't be true. If she had a talking horse, then surely her days of being poor would be over. But alas, Velamir just blinked and waited for his training.

"This world is twisted, Velamir. We have barely enough money to get by. We owe more than we make, and the abominations who could eat us in two seconds are the ones with unending riches. How is that fair?"

Velamir shook his head, rattling the bridle.

Seraphina checked the saddle's fastenings again. "I don't agree that the only way for our family to end our debts is for me to marry that slimy Lord Better-Than-Everyone-Else, and why push me into Venom and Vows? Surely, Father doesn't really think I could win a sponsorship. Or ..." Seraphina tapped her chin, forming a thought. "Maybe Father does believe I can get a sponsorship, so when I'm forced into that horrendous marriage, I enter it on even terms, possibly even our family would hold the higher financial rank."

Seraphina wiped her tear-stained face and snapped her fingers several times, energy flowing through her mind as she considered different possibilities. She kicked over an empty bucket and stood on it, facing Velamir, creating a stage to perform her monologue of philosophies.

She spread her arms wide in the theater of her barn. "We do have to consider the idea of status." She pointed at the geminox, who looked more irritated than intrigued. "We have no status; therefore, Father entered me in Venom and Vows to establish credibility among the flashy elites, so that when I'm forced to begrudgingly marry Jared, then I will potentially be welcomed into their posh dinner parties and merry households."

She spun on one foot, bucket wobbling. "But, our delightful little race would be able to pay off our debts and give us enough to rebuild this place, so it can finally operate at a profit, then we wouldn't need a sponsorship from a snobby tick nor a marriage to a pompous weasel."

She jumped from the bucket, dust clouding her feet, and bowed, expecting cheers from her audience. No luck. She nodded at the beast. Seraphina understood—it was time to ride. She grabbed the saddle's horn and clumsily slipped her boot into the stirrup. Holding onto the horn and the back of the saddle, she hoisted herself up and settled herself onto her trusty steed, leather crackling with each move. They made a great team, a champion pair.

Seraphina considered the sun's position; she was taking a big risk by training at this hour, especially with the launch of Venom and Vows happening tonight. She rolled her eyes at the thought. The evening would be full of flaunting, flirting, and using the right fork.

Her hands clenched the reins tighter, hoping to forget the warm sensation of Jared's lips on them. He scared her, but why? He hadn't hurt her, yet he made her feel uneasy. Was she justifying his actions? Was she trying to make her new life more bearable? She hated the questions spinning in her mind, but she desired to choose who she married—was that so much to hope for? If that were the case, then someone should change it.

Anxiety gripped her heart, but before it could do more damage, she kicked her geminox, and the two of them soared like the wind. Riding would give her the peace she needed to face her undeniable, embarrassing evening, where vampires of every sort would be waiting for her.

CHAPTER FOUR

The Stranger

The cold wind hammered against her cheeks, almost tearing the silk scarf that masked her pale face. Seraphina needed to hurry. Her heart raced faster, unsure if her last-minute defiance had sealed her fate. She glanced back, small strands of black hair escaping the wrap, and felt relief when she saw no one was chasing her. The horse's hooves thudded into the snow-covered ground, showing their urgency—the animal's hot breath forming little clouds in the icy air.

Her stomach sank at the sight before her. Rotten luck is all she ever had. Just once—just once, she'd like to experience good luck, but maybe that only existed in the lands of fairies and fae. Here, only the flawless had fortune. Ahead, she could see one carriage with a broken wheel and another overturned. The two must have crashed somehow, but what a disaster of a scene with children crying, horses tied to trees, and traffic blocked by several more carriages and wagons. Crowds of people gathered, tending to the wounded and removing the broken transportation. Normally, she might feel compelled to help, but today was not the day.

Should she risk going around? That could cause suspicion, and she couldn't risk anyone seeing her. Pulling back on the reins, she weighed her options as the horse pawed against the muddy snow. She swallowed her last remaining saliva, blue eyes darting from side to side. There was no choice. Her only course was through the twisting, dark trees, full of mystery and danger.

A soft grunt escaped her; she would have to go around—into vampire territory. More than fearing vampires, she worried about being caught in her rebellious actions and getting a tongue-lashing from her father. She thought her priorities might be misjudged, but her creature was fast—maybe fast enough to dodge any beady vampire eyes.

Seraphina guided the horse's reins to the right, leading the animal down a dark, untouched snowy path. She kicked the geminox hard, both of them high on adrenaline. Together, they could do this; all they needed was to slip through the forest unnoticed by the most dangerous predators in the kingdoms. *Sure, no problem*, she thought.

Her ears perked up at the sinister sound. She thought she heard laughter in the trees. Her eyes shifted from the thick, twisting trunks to their tops, but she saw nothing except the contorted limbs slightly swaying with the gentle breeze. The vampire forest was known for being tricky, so she dismissed the idea that she heard laughter; she couldn't be late ... again.

A huge gray rat darted across the path, scaring the geminox. It reared up on its hind legs, neighing loudly. Seraphina felt herself slip from the saddle, and the reins were yanked from her hands, causing her to fall backward. She landed with a hard thump, crunching into the snow. Before she could complain that the snow should have had the decency to be soft and cushion her fall, she quickly rolled out of the way of her geminox's stomping.

She heard laughter again, but this time it was nearby—and real. It sounded like a man, but that was no human laugh. She scrambled to her feet, grabbed the animal's reins, and petted him to soothe his nerves. She heard a twig snap and jerked her head to the left. Her pupils dilated. Rotten luck, and she was almost out of time.

A tall, muscular physique crept out of the dark, foggy forest. He had long, wavy, golden hair, high cheekbones, and a sharp jawline that seemed capable of cutting through stone. He wore a loose, white linen shirt with the neckline untied, revealing part of his extremely defined chest. Well, there's something she didn't see every day.

Seraphina's cheeks flushed at the sight of the exposed skin. His dark eyes narrowed, but a roguish grin was etched on his face. A quiet gasp escaped her pink lips, although her lips would most likely turn purple any minute. Her hands and feet felt the bite of the cold. Yet, a warmth spread across her chest, and she took in the presence of the force standing at the edge of the forest. This was the vampire known as Nash Everthorne, the wealthiest, most powerful, and most sought-after vampire in all the realms—and she was now standing alone, face-to-face with him.

Why? This vampire never revealed himself to humans. He never even took part with Venom and Vows, but then she remembered—she was on his territory. She had disturbed him. She was in serious trouble. Vampires were feared for what they were and their past. In their long, long history, they had slaughtered thousands, but centuries ago, one vampire stood out and, with more power than all the other vampires could wish for, he established his dominance. With his leadership, he proclaimed a new order and agreement with the humans: venom for blood. Instead of vampires taking what they wanted, they became more civilized, trading their venom for freely given blood. This eventually bloomed into the legendary Venom and Vows event.

"Good evening, rider." Nash's voice sounded like his throat was made of velvet and temptation—a maze waiting for a victim to seize the chance to solve the puzzle.

Seraphina inhaled sharply and firmly gripped the reins. She needed to remember who she was pretending to be. She had to stay in character. Her hand went to her face, where the scarf was still snugly wrapped around her head and face. She was a man. She was a gentleman practicing his riding, training for the race; nothing more.

She nodded her head, hoping this would appease the vampire.

Nash tilted his head, studying her with an intense gaze that made her uncomfortable. "Now, why would you be out in vampire territory at this hour?"

Seraphina didn't want to answer. She was afraid her voice might give her away. She had practiced speaking in a man's voice but was nervous about his intimidating presence, and that exposed skin kept distracting her.

She forced her eyes to look at his chin. She cleared her throat for an unforgettable performance.

"Forgive me, my lord, I simply wish to attend tonight's festivities on time." She attempted to sound as masculine as she could, but she wasn't sure if it was coming through. She noticed Nash's face twitch. "There was a crash of several carriages on the other road, so I needed to take this route. I hope it's okay that I continue onward without disturbing you."

Nash sniffed the air. She feared he could smell her lies like one of those elder fae. The predator stepped closer. "You're awfully small for such a creature." He gestured to her pet. "Tell me, how did you come by a geminox?"

CHAPTER FIVE

The Geminox

Seraphina froze. This was a lie she wasn't prepared to defend. Her head snapped toward her horse. Darkness flooded her veins as she realized her creature's head covering had fallen off, exposing the azure gem at the center of the animal's head, shining like a lighthouse—except this gem begged for trouble.

A geminox is a hybrid creature, part horse and part unicorn. The law sees it as an abomination, but Seraphina found this young one abandoned and caught in a briar patch. It was left for dead when it was just a newborn. Her heart didn't see an abomination; she saw innocence that needed protection and love. She snuck it to her family's estate and took care of it. She always made sure Velamir wore a head covering, but in the commotion from that stupid rat, it must have fallen off somehow. She made a mental note to return and hunt that wretched varmint.

She opened her mouth to say something, but no words came out. She didn't want the vampire to kill her favorite friend. What was she supposed to do? He would be within his rights to slay it. And how could she stop such a fierce beast? She was no match for a vamp.

Nash chuckled with the same laughter that sent ripples through her body. Why was her own skin betraying her like this? Wasn't her skin supposed to be on her side? She crossed her arms, not wanting him to see how he made her tremble, both from fear and something else.

Nash brushed snow from his shoulder and casually strolled around them, like a lion stalking its prey. "I find it odd that you also have a face covering made of silk. Most men don't wear silk coverings."

She felt her heart skip a beat. Her disguise had several flaws, but silk fabric wasn't one she thought anyone would care about. She should have known better. This was the land of the elitist versus the underprivileged. Of course, a wealthy, snobbish vampire would notice the fabric. Seraphina glared. "Most men aren't like me." She raised her chin. "Once I win the horse race, then it will be the coveted face covering for all horse races."

Nash grinned, revealing his sharp fangs. The moonlight reflected off his pearly white teeth, a beacon of death. "You don't say?"

Nash stepped closer. Snow crunched beneath his shiny black boots. He moved as if he were walking on air—light and effortless. Yet Nash was anything but weightless; his bulging muscles strained against his shirt, and Seraphina found herself wishing they would break free.

Why did this skulking beast get under her skin? She scolded herself. Vamps were varmints just like that stupid rat.

He moved closer, almost a foot away, and sniffed the air again. *Why did he do that?* It irritated her, as if he were playing with her. She hated his kind. He stared into her eyes, never blinking. He tilted his head, assessing her. She felt like he was peering through her, seeing everything she kept hidden from the world. Vamps and their stupid tricks. He reminded her of a spider, and she felt like she was caught in his web.

"I think you may be the best-smelling man I've ever smelled."

Soap! She used her mother's lavender soap earlier today. She couldn't help herself. Soap was the one pleasure her mother had before she became ill, so Seraphina always made sure she bathed with her mother's favorite. But now, her one indulgence could jeopardize her future.

"Please, Your Grace, I need to be on my way for tonight's festivities. I trust you are not attending Venom and Vows?" she said with a question in her male-sounding words.

Nash Everthorne was known for avoiding the annual showcase. He always opted not to sully himself by involving a human household. Instead, Everthorne chose his human blood through other means. Ah, yes, the other caveat to securing a vampire's sponsorship—they obtain your blood without resistance, a willing lamb for their bloodthirsty feast.

Because he kept his venom to himself, his business dealings made him the wealthiest vampire in history, their long history. Rumors suggested Nash was involved in black-market deals and could be seen making shady handshakes at Bloodmist Cove. No one who valued their life would ever venture there, as only greedy goblins, foolhardy fae, and pigheaded pirates were the plagues of that port.

Nash Everthorne usually attended social gatherings and parties, but he avoided Venom and Vows. He was once interviewed and quoted in Heedmoor's newspaper, stating, "When I find someone who piques my interest enough in her daily life, then I'll attend the showcase, but so far, I've only seen ordinary."

Nash stared at Seraphina's boots for too long, then reached out his hand and twirled a long strand of her midnight-black hair around his finger. Her mind went blank. She hated vampires—what they were and how they lived. Their entire existence felt wrong, yet his eyes, his scent, his body... everything about him drew her in. It was a predator's natural biology—a moth to a flame, a fly to the web. Why was she such a reckless bug?

A cunning smile formed across Nash's porcelain face. "Actually, I think this year I will attend. I look forward to seeing you there, rider."

In a blur of snowflakes and cold air, Nash Everthorne was gone, leaving Seraphina with only the long, dark strand of hair blowing across her eyes. She held her hair, the evidence of a law-breaking charade, as reality hit her. Did he know? If he did, why didn't he reveal her? Was he planning to reveal her tonight?

She couldn't focus on that. Seraphina smacked her cheeks. The law stated that women were not allowed to partake in horse racing, not to mention she had crossed into vampire territory without permission; two laws broken in one day. What an achievement! No. He didn't know. If he did, he would have killed her seconds ago, as the generous law permits, but he didn't. Her secret was safe.

She needed to leave—she had wasted too much time talking to the smug vampire. She quickly grabbed Velamir's head covering and secured it to the creature. She paused, looking at her forbidden pet. Nash might not know about her treachery of impersonating a man, but he did know about her treachery of harboring a geminox, so why did he let this creature live? *What game was he playing?*

CHAPTER SIX

The Launch

Borrowed. Everything around her was borrowed to make it seem like the Halloways still had money. The carriage was from Ms. Hatley. The horses came from Mr. Brown's stables, and even the coachman, footman, and young carriage attendant were all Mr. Brown's stable boys pretending to hold noble positions. Everyone agreed to keep this secret because if Seraphina received sponsorship, then all three families would benefit, as they shared certain properties.

Seraphina squirmed in her pearly white dress, wishing she could loosen the unbearably itchy corset and feel relief from the cold air for once. She focused on the cobwebs hanging from the corners of the worn carriage, a foreshadowing of what she was about to face—a sticky web of spidery vampires ready to devour their meals. She only wished she could be a broom and sweep them all away.

"You look lovely, sister," Simon said.

Seraphina offered her brother a small smile, which did little to quiet the butterflies fluttering in her stomach. She fidgeted with the long satin gloves pulled above her elbows, avoiding eye contact with her father. Their dispute still burned inside her, one she felt that would continue.

Seraphina wore her mother's high empire-waist gown, decorated with newly added embroidered floral motifs and voluminous puff sleeves that were fitted at the shoulder and ended near the elbow. Her heart stopped when she felt the carriage stop.

A rigid tapping was heard at the door. "Is this Miss Seraphina Halloway's carriage?" a voice asked.

Seraphina's father opened the door to a short, plump woman with rosy cheeks and nose, wearing a golden gown that revealed way too much of her bosom. Simon and Seymour stifled a laugh.

"It is, mum. I'm her father, Sir Sebastian Halloway."

The woman huffed and crossed her arms, which only strained the seams of her bodice. "You're late! All the other young ladies are already in line to be announced." She started walking toward a side entrance of the enormous mansion where the carriage was parked. "Follow me, Miss Halloway. There's no time to lose."

Sebastian stepped out of the carriage and offered his daughter his hand. Seraphina moved cautiously, her heels crunching on the small, snow-covered pebbles lining the large circular forecourt. The two followed behind the woman in charge of the ladies, while the brothers went inside the mansion through the main door.

Seraphina glanced over her shoulder, catching the last rays of sunset that painted the sky behind the three-tiered fountain.

Instead of water flowing, the fountain was covered in ice, making the unicorn statue appear more ethereal. Her eyes moved forward sharply as the lady knocked on a black iron door.

"This is where you leave her, Sir Halloway."

Sebastian nodded. He leaned in and kissed Seraphina's cheek. "Good luck tonight, my darling. Keep your head high."

What could she say in response to her father? She had no words that could comfort him because they all knew her chances of securing a vampire would be smaller than a ladybug's nose. Before she realized it, he was gone, and all she was left with was the heavy dread forming in her belly. She turned and faced the impatient woman.

"I'm Lady Margreet Hamilton. I'll be guiding you through the events of the evening."

The door swung open, and a wave of warm air and a potent scent of roses assaulted Seraphina's face like the essence of a funeral. She nearly gagged, but all the kingdoms knew vampires favored roses, especially red ones. Something else Seraphina loathed. She didn't like the color red, nor did she enjoy roses. The iris was her favorite flower, and midnight blue was her preferred color.

Before she finished her steps up the red-carpeted staircase, Seraphina could hear them before she saw them: a crowd of cackling hens, all vying to be chosen. She sighed, wishing this miserable night would end. When she reached the top, her mouth fell open at the sea of white gowns.

How was anyone supposed to stand out? Well, she figured that was the game, wasn't it? Perform and outdo your competition, all while looking the same. Vampire scum. She didn't want to be a dancing puppet for those vile creatures. An orchestra of strings sounded, and her shoulders jumped at the music.

Tap. Tap. Tap. Lady Hamilton beat her fan on the banister, capturing every lady's attention. "Listen up, ladies. You will be announced in the order that we've arranged." She peered through the cloud of white to find Seraphina. "Miss Halloway, since you arrived so late, you will be last." The other girls snickered. "Now, it's very important to remember your training and how this evening will go. Once you're announced, you will proceed down the grand staircase and join the guests. Continue walking among the crowd. Do *not* stop unless one of them ..." She cleared her throat, clearly uncomfortable saying the word *vampire*. "... stops you. They may want to speak with you. If they do, then don't ruin your opportunity to impress with conversation."

Seraphina dropped her head. Seeing a vampire was already intimidating, but talking with one was even worse. She remembered how Nash made her feel. *Nash.* She had forgotten about their encounter. She had been distracted by sneaking back into her home, changing into her gown, and presenting herself to her family, not to mention the long journey to the mansion. Was Nash downstairs waiting to reveal her secret?

The room began to spin, and her breathing quickened. She had to regain control before a panic attack took over. She made herself focus on Lady Hamilton's words.

"Drinks will be handed out to you, but I always advise caution. Our hosts can handle alcohol much more easily than we can. My formula is one glass of champagne per two glasses of water."

Seraphina heard whispers and giggles. She noticed girls making faces and shaking their heads. Obviously, some were planning to ignore the advice of their trusted leader, like a child reaching to touch a forbidden fire. Clearly, she was up against professionals. Her lip gave a slight uptick at her private sarcasm toward the ladies.

"I will let you know when it's time to start." Lady Hamilton took her position down the curved staircase on the opposite side of where Seraphina had just ascended. She wondered where this wide walkway led—most likely to countless bedrooms.

She maneuvered to her position at the back of the line, where a stunning woman with dark skin wearing red eyeshadow and painted red lips greeted her with a warm smile. *How clever.*

Seraphina offered back her best attempt at a warm greeting, "Good evening, I'm Seraphina Halloway."

"Wonderful to make your acquaintance, Lady Halloway."

"Oh, no. It's just Miss, not lady." Seraphina dropped her head, cheeks blushing.

Smooth, satin-gloved fingers lifted her chin. "None of that. You must think of yourself as a lady to gain ladyship."

Wow. Seraphina liked this girl already.

"I'm Lady Clara Pemberton."

"Pemberton. As in, *the* Pembertons?" Seraphina asked with astonishment.

Clara waved her hand. "You flatter me, but don't be fooled by a name and title. We like to have fun just like the rest of society."

Seraphina was in shock. The Pembertons had been blessed with sponsorship for the past seventy years, and Clara was a shoo-in for another year. Their family had never known a day's hardship, but they were one of the kind elites, one of very few.

Seraphina's thoughts were interrupted by squeals and high-pitched whispers. She saw most of the girls engaged in frantic gossip. *What were they discussing?* Was it about her? Could she already be the subject of ridicule?

She leaned in to Clara. "Do you know what everyone is whispering about?"

A wide grin flashed across Clara's ebony face. "Ever since this morning, the whole kingdom is flourishing with the same news."

Seraphina's heart pounded, ready for her downfall.

"His Grace, Nash Everthorne, is attending tonight's launch." A cold shiver went down Seraphina's spine. "My mother had a maid deliver me a note an hour ago, telling me he had arrived. I've never met him, but I've heard such stories."

Seraphina thought her heart was going to burst from her chest; she could barely breathe.

"Wha-What stories?" Seraphina stumbled over her words.

"Well, there are the ones everyone knows, like he's the richest vampire in history. He's somehow even the most powerful, too. He's refused a wife, which makes all the female vamps incredibly jealous and angry. My sponsor said she tried for years before she married her husband to get Nash interested, but he never would give in to her advances."

Seraphina's head tilted. "Wait. Your sponsor is a female?"

Clara chuckled. "Yes. Do you not know how this works?" Seraphina shook her head slightly. "It's okay, I will explain. A female vampire can sponsor if she is married. Her mate can choose the same lady or someone else. The problem with that is shared fortunes, which is why Nash's appearance tonight has stirred up quite a bit of excitement. Whoever can land His Grace will have his full sponsorship."

Seraphina was glad that all the ladies would focus their attention on Nash. This might be her way of preventing him from revealing her secret. He would be too busy. Relief washed over her. Lady Hamilton tapped her fan again and instructed the first lady to descend. With the first shimmering step onto the black-carpeted staircase, Venom and Vows had officially begun, promising wealth and power, but also a blood oath.

CHAPTER SEVEN

The Entrance

Loud buzzing festered in Seraphina's ears along with the lingering touch of Lady Clara Pemberton's hand squeeze. It was finally her turn to descend into the glamorous pit of vipers. She tried to swallow, but her mouth was dry—a clear sign she needed to chug champagne immediately. Her beading sparkled against the candlelit chandeliers, almost allowing Seraphina's lack of status to hide. Lady Hamilton waved her forward.

Seraphina's scuffed white satin shoe touched the first step, and she sucked in a deep breath. She couldn't do this. Who was she fooling? Why did she agree to any of this charade? She was completely out of her depth. She would drown in the misery of her shortcomings. In a field of perfect roses, she was the dandelion weed, a jester among perfection.

Her hand trembled against the railing, and tears welled in her pale blue eyes. She paused briefly to survey the grand room for her family, but all she saw were white gowns mingling with vampires. It was like a dance, yet she didn't know the steps. No one's head snapped up to see her like the crowd did for the other ladies. Her newly appointed title dripped with desperation, a sure way to carve her family's destiny in stone—not if she and Velamir had a say.

Seraphina tried to formulate a plan, pausing on a creaking stair, but not even a sympathetic glance came her way. She heard Lady Hamilton shooing her down. She wanted to turn and run back to their farm, far away from this grotesque display, but then the world stilled.

There, in the farthest corner with his back pressed against the wall, was Nash Everthorne, and his eyes were fixed on hers. Why was he watching her so intently? Was it just her, or did he do that to every lady?

She felt one of her hairpins slipping as she took a few more steps forward. Gracefully, a short strand of her raven-black hair gently curled around her face. She saw Nash pushing himself away from the wall, and a hush fell over the crowd.

How could a single movement from one being command such obedience? Like an axe splitting wood, the crowd parted for Nash as he walked to the bottom of the staircase. Before Seraphina could step off the edge, he lifted his hand to her. She froze, feeling herself start to shake. *Was this it?* The moment he decided to expose her in front of everyone who mattered.

"Good evening, Lady Halloway. Would you do me the great honor of allowing me to escort you to some refreshments?" He flashed his devilish smile toward her, like he had secrets of his own.

What was she supposed to do? Say no? She would be killed on sight, or worse, her family would be banished and shamed to live out their days, starving and homeless, with only blankets of snow and pillows of ice. No, she would have to take the hand of a monster to protect herself and her family.

She slipped her silky glove into the strong hand of a man who would much rather gulp down her blood than entertain social graces. "How kind of you, Your Grace."

He guided her through the sea of people, all staring. Whispers swirled around the room like wind rustling leaves. Seraphina's heart pounded, making it hard to hear the music. Her eyes darted around the ballroom, which was trimmed in sparkling gold to match the floor. Red roses decorated every vase and all the table space not covered in hors d'oeuvres and sugary treats.

She thought about her brother, broken and moaning in pain. He would love some of these treats. She would make sure to steal a few for her siblings before the evening ended. Nash stopped in front of the champagne table, grabbing two crystal glasses filled with bubbling golden liquid, a tonic for her nerves.

She accepted the glass he handed her and eyed him as he playfully clinked their glasses and sipped his drink, not taking his dark eyes off her. Seraphina quickly took a small sip, hoping salvation was at the bottom of the glass. He moved closer, too close. Her breath caught.

Two other male vampires approached, one with dark hair, opening his mouth, but before he could speak, Nash snapped, "No. Go away." They recoiled and backed away, disappearing into the puppet show.

Without considering the consequences, Seraphina blurted out, "Well, that was rude."

Nash tilted his head, a smile tugging at his lips. Reality hit Seraphina's nerves as she realized the confrontation she had just directed at the highest-ranking being in all their kingdoms. With one snap, she could be dead, yet she scolded the beast like a child. What was wrong with her?

"Pardon my bewilderment, my lady. No one has ever spoken to me like that." He began to take a sip but paused before the glass could reach his lips. "Well, no one left alive, that is." He chuckled to himself and finished the remaining contents of his champagne.

Seraphina felt her spine shiver, but wait ... *did Nash Everthorne just tell a joke?* Surely not. Vampires were serious creatures—lurking in the dark, obsessed only with their blood quotas. No, of course, Nash wouldn't have a sense of humor. She sipped her drink, trying to suppress her constant habit of blurting out her unwelcome opinions.

"Pity. I'm sure those lost souls and I would have much to converse about," Seraphina said, then slightly gasped.

Well, now she was done. She ended her life with an insult to the most feared vampire, but instead of meeting death in Nash's eyes, she saw crinkles form around his eyes. He was smiling at her. Boots clicking on the floor, Nash stepped closer and took a deep breath next to her ear. Seraphina's breathing quickened.

Nash leaned his golden head back, his gaze crashing into Seraphina's blue eyes like waves pounding against a rocky coastline. "Why, you might be the best-smelling rider I've ever smelled."

CHAPTER EIGHT

The Promise

*H*e *knows. He's known this entire time.* Should she run? How childish. She couldn't outrun a vampire. She tried to say something, anything, but no words came out of her pink lips. Her mind raced to make a plan, but his kind surrounded her, and her people couldn't do anything against the plague of vampires.

Instead of outing her, instead of killing her, instead of banishing her, Nash took her hand and placed it on top of his. "Would you do me the great honor of joining me at my private table?"

What was this game? Her ears burned with fear. She wasn't going anywhere, but they were already moving. She had to do something.

"Please, Your Grace, before my family joins, may I have a private moment with you?"

"Ah, your words found you. Good. You gave me a fright."

A slight laugh fell through her response. "A fright?" she asked incredulously.

"Do you not believe vampires can possess fear?"

"Since that *is* an emotion, no—I didn't think vampires could feel anything." Her free hand flew to her mouth, both embarrassed by her immature behavior and stunned that she had insulted this predator twice in just a few minutes.

She started to apologize, but Nash interrupted, "No need. I'm looking forward to hearing more of those untamed thoughts of yours." He motioned for her to sit at his table in the corner.

Seraphina took the golden chair Nash offered her, allowing him to adjust it closer to the table, which was draped in bright white linen. She scanned the room, seeing other ladies taking their seats at prospect tables. She gulped. They were now to demonstrate their table manners, from engaging in pleasant conversation to using that blasted tiny fork correctly.

She had to act quickly. "Your Grace, you seem to share a familiarity with me that I might not be aware of."

Nash slid his chair closer to the round table and unfolded his white cloth napkin, which had been carefully shaped to resemble a rose. He snapped his fingers, signaling for another champagne, quickly brought by a frantic server. Nash took a long sip, keeping his gaze fixed on her.

As he set his glass down, he let out a dramatic sigh. "Lady Halloway ..."

Seraphina raised her hand above her golden charger. "Oh, it's just Miss, not Lady."

Why did she say that? *The* Clara Pemberton told her not to do exactly what she had just done.

Nash cleared his throat. "In my presence or anyone else's, you will address yourself as Lady. Is this understood?"

Seraphina covered her exposed neckline with her hand and nodded, confused by the kind gesture he just offered.

"And as for the lying ..." Seraphina's cheeks flushed at his words. "Let's not pretend we didn't meet on the road." He flashed her a winning grin.

She began to nod, then suddenly froze. "My—my horse ..."

Nash tilted his head. "Didn't we just establish no lies?"

She couldn't say the word *geminox* with all these people around. She had to play his game. But how could she play a vampire's game, especially when the rules had now all shifted in Nash's favor?

"Of course, Your Grace. What I meant to say was my pet, Velamir." This made Nash smile again. Why did she enjoy seeing him smile? *Was it the crinkles around his eyes or the innocence of a time long forgotten that spilled across his features?* Didn't she remember the past of the vampires: villainous creatures who would steal family members in the night? Or perhaps Seraphina needed to remind herself that these well-dressed leeches had storehouses of gold, hoarded away while her people starved. Well, that did it. She snapped out of the bloodthirsty creature's trance and refocused on her mission.

"I'm concerned for his—well, for his life, Your Grace."

Nash was about to take another sip of his champagne, but instead pondered her words. He set the crystal down, playfully fiddling with the stem. His dark eyes narrowed. "You would ask me first about your pet, rather than ask about your own fate?"

Seraphina thanked the heavens for the server who placed another glass of fizzy liquid in front of her. She quickly snatched the flute and drank every last shimmering trace. She fought the urge to grab her throat; it burned, and her eyes watered. Her belly ached with an unladylike bubble full of desperation for freedom.

Nash's mouth twitched, and Seraphina was amazed. He looked like he was about to burst into laughter at her pain. Nash pressed his lips together before saying, "I'm guessing you're in quite some discomfort now."

Seraphina lifted her chin in defiance. "Not at all, Your Grace. I'm simply on the edge of my seat to hear your answer to my question."

"I'll skip the part where you didn't actually ask me a question at all. You just made a statement, wishing you had asked one." Seraphina glared. "Easy, Lady Halloway. Your pet is safe from me, as is your other little secret—as long as you continue to tell the truth."

"I will if you will." The words burst from Seraphina's mouth like a geyser erupting. She opened her mouth to apologize, but caught a particular look in his eyes—an expression that seemed to show pleasure. *Was this what it took to win Nash's sponsorship: honest conversation?*

Movement disturbed Nash and Seraphina. The ladies' families gathered at the tables, causing Nash to grimace when Seraphina's brothers sat in the empty chairs around his table. Seraphina wondered why this would bother him when he knew what would happen next. No matter. Her next battle was clear: the table setting.

Why do these elites need so many forks? She tried to recall the studies from her youth, but her memories were hazy. Without warning, Lady Hamilton clapped her hands, causing a flood of servers to glide gracefully through the clusters of tables, and there sat in front of Seraphina her enemy—potted shrimps on toast rounds accompanied by pickled quail eggs and herbed cucumber slices. How in all the blazing fires was she supposed to eat this?

And then, the vampire with dazzling fangs did something unexpected.

CHAPTER NINE

The Time of Day

Gleaming silver in the flickering candlelight, Nash twirled his fish fork and fish knife, tilting his head at Seraphina. Was he helping her? Why would a vampire assist a lady trying to impress him? Wasn't this the very definition of how the evening shouldn't go?

Seraphina quickly grabbed the utensils and watched Nash's movements, studying his precise way of cutting and stabbing the food. He ate so benevolently, not like the ravenous monster she expected. Well, maybe that's because this food was cooked, not streaming with hot blood. Vampires—human mosquitoes.

She could see Nash growing bored of her family's stories, so she, as the lady she was, took her napkin, held it to her mouth, dabbed her lips, and cleared her throat—clearly, the formal and polite way of signaling that the conversation should end. But, of course, Seraphina only had bad luck, and what was meant to be a ladylike throat clearing was nothing more than the previous troublesome discomfort waiting for just such an opportunity to surface.

Seraphina looked at her father with her mouth wide open like a fish. Her face burned, and her head spun. She had burped in public at a dinner table with the richest vampire as her witness. She could have hiccupped or sneezed, but no—her treacherous body found her first public belching should come at this exact, perfect moment.

She jerked her head toward Nash. "My apologies, Your Grace. I'm ever so ..."

Nash waved his hand. "No need, my dear. At least, it was honest." The powerful vampire lowered his head, not able to hide his smile.

Seraphina almost chuckled. *Did the two of them just share an inside joke?* She had stumbled her way through every point of tonight, yet now she had a secret with Nash, an intimate secret.

Nash ignored the brothers' laughing and stared into Seraphina's eyes. "Lady Holloway, what is your favorite time of day?"

The fun drained from her face. Once again, Nash was playing a game where the rules kept changing. He had saved her from embarrassment at every turn and made her promise not to lie, so why would he ask this question?

Since girls first learn to speak, they are taught that a lady's favorite time of day is mid-morning, right after breaking her fast, when the sun is still rising and the temperature is perfect for a walk or relaxing in the gardens. The trick, however, is that she promised Nash no lies, and that regurgitation of malarkey was most certainly not her favorite.

She sat like a stiff corpse in her chair. She could hear the other girls repeating the same phrase she had been taught. She knew the words, but Nash was skilled at detecting lies, too skilled. Her brothers' puzzled expressions didn't surprise her. They had grown up hearing the same phrase drilled into them.

But she promised—no lies.

"My favorite time of day is ..." She paused and looked around the room again, then focused on Nash's broody brow. He beckoned, no—he commanded the truth. And she found herself waiting to obey. "Well, it's at night, Your Grace."

Her brothers slammed their backs into their chairs too dramatically, while her father downed the last of his champagne.

Nash straightened and leaned forward. "At night?" He lifted his chiseled jaw. "Go on, why?"

Seraphina swallowed, hoping she wasn't condemning her family to eternal ruin. "I—I like the stars, Your Grace. Their shimmering mysteries against a dark canvas make me feel like the heavens are playing a symphony just for me. I know that might sound silly, but in that moment, I feel special. I feel seen because it's in the darkness that I can truly be myself. I only wish I could dance among the stars, moving to their melodies, free of prying eyes, and void of any imperfections."

The table remained silent for a long time. The servers even took up the first course and brought out the second before Nash spoke.

"Forgive me, my lady. It's not often that I'm rendered speechless. I found your honesty to be most stirring."

They proceeded in silence with each course; Seraphina quietly coached on utensils and table manners from the human mosquito, but the atmosphere changed after several vampires dressed in black approached Nash, whispering continuously in his ear. Then, he would give them hushed instructions, shooing them away.

Seraphina felt a sugar rush from her second helping of the pomegranate syllabub. She reached for a third scoop from the glass goblet but lost her nerve when she saw another secret exchange between those vampires.

"My apologies, Your Grace."

Lingering to Nash's right, the stranger vampire stiffened. Nash's brow furrowed.

"Why do you apologize?"

Seraphina twirled her spoon in her dessert. "Clearly, we are boring you, and you'd rather be involved with whatever scheming situation is obviously happening."

Her father raked his hand over his wrinkled face. "Seraphina," he hissed.

Something cold flashed across Nash's face, but it immediately vanished behind a look that suggested he'd won a poker hand he wasn't supposed to. He leaned back in his chair and strummed his fingers on the white linen, nails perfectly maintained. "The first associate briefed me about a business deal I was supposed to attend this evening, but my plans changed, rather abruptly."

Seraphina shifted in her chair. She felt like a schoolgirl receiving a lecture from her teacher.

"The second was giving me a report on how the healer performed on your brother's leg."

"What?" Seraphina asked a bit too loudly for a lady.

"Ah, yes. When your brothers regaled me with the tales of your younger siblings and the injury, I sent a healer to help."

"But, Your Grace, that would cost … that would cost more than …" Sebastian choked on his words, not wanting to utter the shame and humiliation that he was trying to conceal.

Nash slightly raised his hand. "Please, Sir Halloway. You owe me nothing. The healer simply owed me a favor, and this seemed the best way for her to pay it."

Seraphina watched Nash's gaze settle on her. Her breaths came deep and steady. He knew more than he was revealing now. The healer had seen inside their home, a crumbling, nearly empty place. Tears of anger and betrayal threatened to spill from her sapphire eyes.

"The third associate was the head chef for the evening. I instructed him to pack up all the leftovers and have them preserved and packed in a wagon outside." The Halloways each showed confused expressions. "This last gentleman …" He patted the vampire's arm, who looked like he had swallowed a bug—a terrible-tasting bug. "… is Arnaelo. I've asked him to take the wagon to your home."

Seraphina slammed her hand on the table, making the silverware rattle against the china. "How dare you!"

Anger burned in Nash's eyes. "How dare I?"

"Yes. We don't need your pity, nor do I want it. You had no business going to our home. You didn't ask; you just did it because you could."

With his eyebrows pushing toward the sky in astonishment, Nash wiped his mouth as a gentleman would before a scolding. "And I guess I was just supposed to ignore the scraps of food that you kept sneaking under the table, or was I not supposed to see that?"

Servers delivered the final course of coffee and marzipan bonbons, hoping to stay out of the lively conversation at Nash's table.

Seraphina looked down into her lap at her makeshift bag made from her napkin, filled with half-eaten pieces of food. Her lip quivered, and a tiny tear slipped from her icy eye as she noticed Nash's unwavering scrutiny. Nash stood abruptly, the chair scraping loudly against the floor. He tossed his napkin onto the plate, nodded at Arnaelo, and bowed to the Halloways, then proceeded to walk out the door without looking back.

She heard the wind of whispers begin, but instead of watching the others, she swiftly began gathering the bonbons into her napkin. Arnaelo glided over to her and gently placed a hand on hers.

"There's no need, my lady. Your brother, Shiloh, mentioned they were his favorites, so His Grace ordered not only for the leftovers from tonight to be packed up but also a fresh barrel a month for him."

"What?" Seraphina asked in a gasp.

"Oh, and Miss Sophia gave very strict instructions that if her brother received bonbons, then she must have the pomegranate syllabub."

A small grin tugged at Seraphina's lips. Her little sister had only ever had pomegranate syllabub once, and it was by accident. Someone thought she was the little girl who had ordered it when she walked into a luxury restaurant. She took it and ran to catch up with the rest of the family, and no one stopped her.

Throughout the entire journey home, she talked about how she could eat this one treat every day.

"His Grace made sure that pitchers would be delivered of her choice."

"But why? I thought he hated me?"

"Hated? My lady, no. You entertained him."

Seraphina's blood boiled. *Why that cocky, self-centered, generous monster!*

CHAPTER TEN

The Invitation

The next morning, the Halloways looked in wonder at the piles of food on their worn wooden table. Her nose was filled with delicious smells of crispy bacon, fluffy biscuits, and steaming eggs. Seraphina almost didn't want to touch the scene; surely, disturbing such an emotional picture of beauty was a crime. She saw the joy across her siblings' faces and, without thinking, she plucked a plump grape and threw it at Shiloh.

He smiled and laughed. "Hey! No fair." Shiloh quickly grabbed two grapes and returned the gesture.

"Children. Children," Sebastian scolded. "Settle down. Just because there's plenty here doesn't mean we should waste it. Let's break our fast in peace and happiness. And no weapons of grapes."

They all expressed their blessings and eagerly indulged in the masterpiece without a hint of guilt in the air. Seraphina replayed the events of the previous night once more, as she had done repeatedly. She couldn't hold back her emotions. One moment she believed she had ruined her life, and the next she thought that a vampire could actually be kind—*kind!*

What foolish thinking! After hearing she was just his entertainment, she felt embarrassed—embarrassed for believing they could form a genuine friendship, embarrassed for risking her life solely so a creature could laugh and sneer at her, and embarrassed that he secretly brought people to her home and showed them pity, enough to shower them with food for months.

But then she looked into her family's faces, and a wave of relief washed over her. They wouldn't go hungry. Today, Father would work the fields with a full belly. Shiloh and Sophia could run in the gardens without feeling faint. She wanted to sob with happiness, but everything shattered when they heard a bell ringing.

Their only servant, who worked part-time, entered the feasting room with wide eyes and a worried expression. Her dirty hand trembled as she handed the letter to Seraphina. Seraphina's mouth dropped open. A letter. A letter for her, but who ... her heart dropped into her stomach as she flipped the envelope over to the P stamped into the red wax. P for Pemberton. She tore the letter open, anxiety and excitement rushing through her fingers.

"Come on, Sera," Shiloh pleaded. "Don't keep us in the dark."

"Yes! What does it say?" squeaked Sophia.

Seraphina wasn't sure what shade of pale she turned, but she guessed moonlight was probably the right color because Lady Clara Pemberton had just invited her for tea this afternoon at Pemberton Place—only the largest mansion in Heedmoor ... a minor detail. Seraphina swallowed her gasp.

Like the good brother he was, Simon snatched the letter and began to read aloud, "Lady Clara Pemberton requests the pleasure of your presence for tea at Pemberton Place this afternoon at three o'clock."

A loud squeal erupted from Sophia, followed by her shoving her chair and bouncing up and down next to Seraphina. "May I come? May I come? Please. Please. Please!"

Sebastian swallowed another sip of coffee, already shaking his head. "Of course, you cannot. This invitation is for ladies of society."

"But Sera's not a Lady," Sophia protested.

Clara and Nash's words came flooding back, almost like a forgotten memory. "Actually, according to Lady Pemberton and his supreme smugness, Lord Everthorne, I am a Lady, and you best start treating me like one." She started poking her sister's belly, which earned her another squeal and a laugh.

Right on time with the mood-damping, Seymour interjected, "What will you wear, Lady Halloway?"

Seraphina didn't miss the bitterness dripping from his question. Why wasn't her brother grateful? He had just eaten the most delicious spread, yet he taunted her.

Unfortunately, as she looked at her regular farming clothes, she realized he wasn't wrong in asking the pondering question. What did a "lady" of her status wear to tea?

Seraphina looked into her father's eyes. "Do you think Ms. Hatley would have something I could borrow, or perhaps we have something here she could fix?"

There was no mistake in the sparkle of Sebastian's eyes at the sound of Ms. Hatley's name. "I think that's a wonderful idea. I'll saddle up our horse and ride over there to find out."

All the children looked at one another, giggling and passing sly looks.

"When are you two going to give up this charade?" Simon asked, lips smiling.

"Oh, come now, Father. It's impossible not to see how much the two of you adore each other. There's no secret she feels the same about you." Seraphina plucked a grape with a loud snap and playfully popped it into her mouth, daring her father to deny the love he had for their neighbor.

Sebastian stood, chair grinding. "What I think is that you young ones have much more exciting lives to live than focusing on simple matters of your old father." With a wink, he left for the stables.

After several hours of riding Velamir, Seraphina reluctantly decided to return home to the busy scene of several dresses hanging throughout her room, while Ms. Hatley and Anna, the servant, were sewing final touches onto one of Seraphina's mother's old dresses. She saw her mother's dusty trunk, which must have weighed a great deal and smelled ancient.

"Oh, Seraphina, I mean, Miss Halloway, or should I say Lady?"

Seraphina placed her hand on Ms. Hatley's sweaty shoulder. "Seraphina will do nicely." She looked down at the pale seafoam fabric, adorned with a light, sheer overlay embroidered with white roses. She ran her hand over the pearly satin ribbon stitched underneath the bust line. "I know my mother's dresses, and this is not one... how?" She could only utter that one word before a waterfall of tears spilled.

Sophia sprang from behind a moth-eaten mannequin. "Well, we cut the sheer overlay from that pink dress over there and removed the only white ribbon we could find that didn't have some type of yellow stain on it from this red dress."

"Quite right, Sophia," Ms. Hatley praised. "The overlay over this seafoam dress was badly marked, so I cut it away. There may still be some parts that I could use for a hat or an accent for sleeves. For now, I believe this will be a wonderful dress for you to wear."

Ms. Hatley stood and held the dress up for Seraphina to examine. Seraphina was hesitant to touch it with her unwashed hands.

"It's stunning. You all could be the fashion designers for the vampires."

The ladies cooed and blushed at the embellished compliment, but Seraphina took pride in their achievement. She would wear this dress with honor. She hurried to the wash chamber, gasping at the cold water, and scrubbed until her skin was red. Today, she was excited to smell her mother's soap. She dried herself with a rough towel and slipped all the layers of her costume over her pale skin, feeling like her family's doll.

"You'll take my carriage again." Ms. Hatley took Seraphina's hands and placed long white gloves in them, then she nodded to Sophia, who beamed, knowing it was now her turn to surprise her sister.

Sophia carefully placed an intricately carved wooden box on the bed beside Seraphina and opened it, hinges creaking against rust. Seraphina's hand moved to her mouth. Her mother's pearl necklace—she thought it had been lost. Tears welled up in her eyes as she embraced her sister tightly.

"We found it hidden in the red dress. Did you know that was Mother's last day of Venom and Vows dress?"

Seraphina tilted her head at the deep crimson gown, a dress that wanted to sparkle and wanted to dazzle a crowd once more, but Seraphina hated the color red. In fact, she never wanted red to ever touch her skin—after all, wasn't that the favored color of vampires? *Vicious creatures.*

She snapped her head out of the trance. "I'm certainly glad you found it. The pearls will match perfectly. Thank you all so much for this dress."

"No more dawdling, it's time for you to go," Ms. Hatley said, guiding Seraphina out the door and to the carriage.

With Anna as her chaperone, the two traveled in silence to the grandeur of Heedmoor as they passed through the tall, arched gates and onto the smooth, stone streets. They listened to the horses' hooves clicking and the bustle of people chatting near the long row of white marble shops trimmed in gold.

Seraphina nearly pressed her face against the window of the carriage, watching the scenes as they drove by. Pastry shops displayed colorful desserts, making her mouth water, followed by the thought that she had forgotten to eat before leaving. Modistes showcased their most fashionable dresses, and milliners exhibited pristine hats and caps, some of which even looked like ice castles.

She watched men dressed in their high-fashion suits, tipping their tall hats as ladies in pale pink and pearly white dresses giggled at the flirtations. She stared in awe as their maids walked behind carrying stacked boxes, undoubtedly filled with the riches of any elite's wardrobe.

Seraphina leaned back, exhausted from witnessing a society where she didn't belong, and sighed. What was she doing? Why did she accept this invitation? Suddenly, her questions ended as the carriage came to a stop. Her door opened to reveal a limestone mansion that soared into the clouds, with multiple pointed towers reaching high into the sky.

She dared to step over the threshold into the masquerade. When she entered Lady Clara Pemberton's drawing room, her blood ran cold, for Clara was not alone. Sitting on the rose velvet couches were the Pembertons' vampires.

The female vampire stood, almost like she moved through water. Her chocolate hair touched the back of her thighs, and her lips were stained red. Her piercing gaze felt like daggers—a good, welcoming sign. She scrutinized Seraphina from head to toe, then locked eyes with her.

"We were just visiting from our mansion for our ..." She paused and looked at Clara. "Exchange." She flashed her fangs, then jerked her head toward Seraphina, eyes piercing. She sucked her teeth loudly. "Well, this is the famous Lady Seraphina Halloway, the one and only woman to ever capture the attention of Nash Everthorne. How ever did you manage that?"

CHAPTER ELEVEN

The Threat

And what do you do when you're surrounded by beasts that seem eager to eat you? Bears: back away slowly and try to look large, that's what her father told her. Wolves: stay calm and speak firmly. *But a vampire?* Perhaps pretend to be innocently stupid.

"Forgive me, but I don't know what you mean?" Seraphina hoped that would buy her some time to figure out an escape plan. How could Clara do this to her? She had hoped to make one friend, but this was a betrayal.

"Oh my," the female vampire said while placing her hand on her chest. "She's dim-witted and featherbrained."

There it was—the nerve the vampire decided to pluck. "Now, wait a minute," Seraphina started.

Standing, Lady Clara intervened, "Friends, let's sit and enjoy simply getting to know Lady Halloway."

Servants rushed in, arranging a selection of freshly baked sponge cakes, biscuits, and macaroons along with tea and coffee. Seraphina sat, observing the masterpiece of sustenance before her. This was Clara Pemberton's daily life. She wondered if the Lady knew how blessed she was.

Clara lightly cleared her throat, beckoning the servants to serve the vampires, then everyone else. "So, Lady Halloway, tell us about yourself. You must have many stories."

Seraphina's heart raced. What should she say? What shouldn't she say? Would this reflect poorly on her chances with Venom and Vows?

"I'm afraid there's not much to tell." She heard the female vampire snicker. "We live a different life in the country."

Seraphina didn't want to feel embarrassed by her family, so why was she suddenly feeling insecure about who she was and where she came from? Vampires. Vampires and their ridiculous, snobby traditions, wandering their private island and trapping humans in their version of existence—she would not let these blood-sucking mosquitoes tarnish her wonderful family.

She sipped her tea and smiled. "But I will say that my family grows the sweetest spinach you'll ever taste, and my brother, Seymour, is probably the most intelligent human in all the lands. He's exceptionally brilliant with figures, but my eldest brother, Simon, is as strong as an ox. I once saw him carry three bales of hay by himself! Shiloh and Sophia, twins, are the youngest and the fullest of life and mischief. Shiloh is the champion of skipping rocks, and Sophia seems to always adopt pregnant cats, so our farm constantly has brand new kittens."

Seraphina almost laughed at the expressions on the vampires' faces. They probably had never heard such words spoken in their cold presence.

"Um, well, wow. Your life sounds splendid," Clara said. "You have such a big family. How wonderful."

"Father said if my mother hadn't died, then they probably would have had more. She loved children."

Clara's face softened. "Oh, Seraphina, I'm so sorry to hear this. My condolences."

Seraphina nodded. "Thank you, but it's been a while now. Enough time that I believe my father has a new love interest in our neighbor. We're all excited and waiting for them to admit it."

Seraphina couldn't believe it—Clara was laughing. *Was this what friendship looked like? Sharing information and enjoying each other's company?*

"This sounds like those gossip columns we read about in the daily paper. Arissa loves to read them." Clara nudged the female vampire's arm.

Arissa, was it? Good to know that formal introductions would now be inferred from context clues. Seraphina observed the interactions between Arissa and Clara. *Arissa seemed to like Clara, so why was she so opposed to her?*

Commotion stirred outside the drawing room. Arissa and her partner stood fast, too fast. Something wasn't right. Seraphina looked at Clara, who looked just as confused and just as scared as she was. *What was happening?* Would this be her way to escape?

The doors burst open, and in walked Nash Everthorne, rage festering on his face.

"Your Grace," squeaked Clara, who immediately stood and bowed.

Seraphina looked at the vampires exchanging silent arguments. She slowly stood and gave a forced bow to Nash. "Your Grace," she said, feeling like her tongue had just licked dirt.

"Do you think this is a game, Arissa?" Nash yelled.

"Don't you speak to her that way, Nash," the not-yet-introduced vampire said.

"Shut it, Steavan. I'll speak however I choose, especially to one who likes to play games."

Steavan turned to Arissa. "What did you do?"

Arissa crossed her arms over her crimson dress and sat with an attitude against the couch. "I may have sent Nash an invitation to this gathering."

Nash advanced towards the vampires, also edging nearer to Seraphina, almost as if he was protecting her. *Surely not.* Seraphina watched his hands tense and relax, and a flutter of emotion stirred inside her as she ran her eyes over the veins bulging on his skin. *What in all of Heedmoor was that about?*

"You're leaving out the threat," Nash snapped.

"Threat?" Steavan threw his hands up. "Arissa!"

"Relax. It was only a joke."

"Not to me," Nash said in almost a growl. Seraphina shuddered.

Arissa rose and, with unnatural speed, stood nose to nose with Nash, who didn't flinch. "Why her? She's completely common and probably still has dirt under her nails from farming spinach. She's entirely incompetent and lacks the talents a lady should have, and ..."

"Enough!" roared Nash. "Make another sound, and I'll send you through that wall. Never insult Lady Halloway or her family again."

Nash started to turn toward Seraphina, but Arissa reached for his arm. "Nash, wait …"

The Nash Everthorne grabbed her hand and bent it backward, bones cracking, sending Arissa to her knees. "Shall I continue to break every bone in your pathetic body?"

Trying not to gag at the disturbing sounds, Seraphina stood and cautiously placed her hand on Nash's shoulder. She felt him shiver and tense. "Please, Your Grace … don't."

"Steavan, take Arissa and leave. Don't even look in Lady Halloway's direction or mine at any other festivities until I say you can."

Steavan nodded. He cradled Arissa in his arms and sped out of the city.

Nash bowed toward Clara. "My apologies, Lady Pemberton. I'm sure your intentions were good, but don't trust Arissa."

"Of course, Your Grace. How can I make this better?"

"By letting me escort Lady Halloway back to her home. I'm sure you ladies need time to prepare for tonight."

Clara smiled and curtsied. Nash extended his arm, and Seraphina hesitantly slipped hers through his. She glanced back and saw Clara, who appeared apologetic, and then they climbed into the most luxurious carriage Seraphina had ever seen.

She settled onto the plush black velvet cushions with ease and traced her fingers along the intricately gold-painted walls that extended to the ceiling. It had a familiar scent. *Was that lavender?* Just like her mother's soap. She cracked a grin.

"Why are you smiling?" Nash asked as he closed the door.

"Because, Your Grace, this might be the best-smelling carriage I've ever encountered."

The two burst into laughter—a laugh shared between friends— and Seraphina realized she enjoyed hearing the sound of the most terrifying creature laughing. She had just seen his cruelty, but now she was giggling like a young schoolgirl with the boy every girl wished she could have. He could ruin everything.

CHAPTER TWELVE

The Fiddle

The carriage felt awkward after the laughter subsided. Seraphina wanted to know what threat Arissa made that would anger Nash so much, but she didn't want to add anything new to her nightmares. Maybe ignorance was best.

She fiddled with her embroidered roses, proud of their origin. "Your Grace," she started. "I wanted to thank you for the food. We shared a lovely meal together this morning, and ... and it ..." she sighed. "Thank you."

Nash's expression softened. "You're most welcome, but you don't need to thank me. It was a gesture long overdue."

The carriage bumped along the road to the countryside, where all the farmers and common folks lived—the place where Arissa would most certainly never be seen. Smells of animal manure and hay drifted into the carriage, reminding Seraphina of home.

Her brow furrowed. "Overdue?"

Nash tilted his head. "The conditions of the outskirts ..."

"Outskirts!"

Nash raised his hand. "I mean no disrespect. It's merely an identification of location."

"In accordance with Heedmoor," Seraphina interrupted. "What if Heedmoor is on the outskirts of the countryside?"

Nash gave a half smile. "Your perspective is unique and one I'll take into consideration." He leaned further back against the plush velvet lining, studying Seraphina.

"You were saying, Your Grace ..."

"Ah, yes. The conditions of the countryside have been neglected for too long. We should do more to support those who bear the responsibility of feeding the cities."

"So, charity?"

Nash's eyes narrowed. "Or maybe your family didn't feel more supported to get their daily tasks done without the—what did you call it? The lovely meal."

Seraphina jerked her head away from Nash's gaze and stared out the window, an insecure sensation creeping over her as she realized they were close to her home. She didn't want him there.

She took a deep breath, trying to calm her anger. "Yes, we enjoyed your leftovers. Now, would you be so kind as to stop the carriage?"

"Stop the carriage?"

"I wish to walk."

"Have I offended you?"

"In every shade and definition of the word, yes."

Nash pounded on the ceiling with his fist, nearly cracking it. The carriage immediately came to a halt. Seraphina didn't wait for assistance. She opened the door, but not before Nash grabbed her arm.

"I don't understand."

"Why would you? We're simply commoners here for your amusement. After all, I'm just your entertainment, right?"

A stunned look flashed across Nash's face, and he let go of her. Clumsily, Seraphina stumbled out of the carriage, preparing to take her walk home. She took a few steps before hearing Nash call out.

"Lady Halloway."

She snapped her head around, prepared to spit more insults at the insect. She saw Nash leaning out the open doorway with sorrowful eyes. *Sorrowful? Again, how could a vampire have any real feelings?*

"I need you to know—there's nothing common about you."

Had she turned to stone? She physically couldn't move from shock, astonished at the kind words. With her mouth hanging open at the ability of a compliment coming from a tyrant's lips, Seraphina watched Nash close the door, and the carriage moved past her, leaving only mud and the most ridiculous thoughts for her comfort.

Seraphina's chair creaked as she shifted once again for the thousandth time during the evening's daunting show, where ladies continued with the second night of Venom and Vows. Tonight highlighted their musical talents. Whether through singing or playing instruments, the women performed, hoping this would be the night they finally caught the attention of a wealthy vampire.

So far, Seraphina had watched ladies play the pianoforte and the harp along with countless songs sung—all with the same posh melodies of the elites, which only made her anxiety grow. The music selection of the countryside was very different from this glittering society. She watched Clara Pemberton take center stage, and the most exquisite chords flowed from her voice.

Seraphina looked down at her black bag, concealing the instrument she had no choice but to play. She sighed and scanned the crowd again, still not spotting Nash. Why did his absence bother her? It wasn't as though she was relying on or hoping for a sponsorship from him. She had other plans for saving her family's farm. But was it so unreasonable to think they had shared a slight friendship? Of course, because she kept insulting him.

She needed to apologize, just like Lady Clara had apologized to her when she had arrived earlier this evening. Arissa's rudeness hadn't even been Clara's fault, but she still owned it, like the wonderful, sweet person she was.

So, if Nash was finally understanding how her people had to live and wanted to bring about change, why should she stand in the way? Her neighbors would only benefit, but her pride and ego had taken a bite out of him. She saw the pain in his dark eyes—a look she never thought a vampire could possess.

Her hands tugged at her fingers, not calming the butterflies in her stomach. *Were these butterflies? They felt more like giant bats!* As Clara's song was ending, Seraphina felt her breath catch as she watched Nash slip in through the corner door—his corner. He didn't even sit down. He leaned against the wall with folded arms, boots crossing.

Great—now, he would bear witness to her humiliation. Seraphina didn't know a single chord on the harp, and what little she knew of the pianoforte was just two or three notes, not a whole song. Her voice, if it could even be called that, sounded like a drunken donkey in song—according to Shiloh. To her bad luck, she was stuck with a commoner's instrument: the fiddle. She loved its sound and music, but aristocratic people didn't dance to the songs she knew, so she fully expected this performance to be like nails upon a chalkboard to their ears.

The crowd clapped and stood, cheering for Clara, and why wouldn't they? She was flawless. Her ebony skin sparkled with bits of diamond dust brushed across her cheeks, and her pale pink eye shadow contrasted beautifully with her chocolate eyes. Even the tiny pink roses in her hair seem to smile at her melodies. Silly plants. Clara took her seat, adjusting the baby pink gloves she and every other lady wore. *Ah, perfection—what better time for a fiddler to perform?*

Seraphina watched Lady Hamilton step into the spotlight to introduce her as the next entertainer. She felt nauseous. Lady Hamilton's hand signaled for Seraphina to come forward. She hadn't heard a word the woman said because her ears were ringing. She leaned over and grabbed her bag, a gesture that earned her whispers.

She looked out over the audience with pleading eyes. Would mercy show up tonight? She hoped, but if not, she prayed for a plague to break out right now. With a click, she released the handle and pulled out the worn fiddle. Gasps and snickers bounced from wall to wall, from chair to chair—except for one vampire, who unfolded his arms and took a few steps away from his concealment.

Seraphina let go of her bag and positioned the fiddle just below her left collarbone, tilting slightly. This position helped tavern fiddlers, who were also her teachers, move around and dance with the crowd. She had only played at family gatherings or local pubs, never on a formal stage. With a trembling right hand, she guided the bow toward the blasphemous contraption.

She closed her eyes and embraced the darkness, her friend who never judged, always applauding with twinkling stars and gentle moonlight. Taking a deep breath, she began with a loud tapping of her shoe. As soon as her bow struck the strings, rough and feral notes exploded through the room, urging listeners' bodies to sway and become one with the energy. She played relentlessly, plunging each soul into her world, where she now commanded them into a pool of shifting tempos.

She didn't open her eyes. She didn't want the distraction of judgmental statues to ruin her masterpiece of woven reels and jigs. This was her time to stand firm against the storm of societal evolution. She was determined that Venom and Vows would not change her ... but then she heard it—a clap, followed by a boot stomp. The crowd joined the one who dared to merge with her raspy dirge of galloping notes.

Seraphina dared to open her icy blue eyes, which soon filled with tears of joy as she watched the entire audience clap, stomp, and some even dance to her fiddling. She played her final chords and bowed to the roaring applause of what she once thought were her enemies. She slipped her pale pink gloves back on after tucking away her fiddle in the bag and took her seat. Clara reached over and squeezed her hand.

"Well done, Lady Halloway."

"Thank you, Lady Pemberton. I think I might be in shock."

Clara giggled. "I believe everyone is in shock."

Doors opened on the crowd's right side, welcoming guests and contestants to follow into the ballroom, which was filled with a display of instruments from throughout Lurin's history and a delicious array of refreshments. Seraphina looked for her family and also found herself searching for Nash. Simon wrapped his arms around Seraphina's waist, startling her. She spun around, smacking his arm while laughing.

"You scared me."

Simon took her hand. "You were remarkable. You had these posh people dancing, Sera ... dancing to our music. You did that."

She blushed, not used to her brother gushing over her. "I honestly was so scared. I was convinced I would be escorted off the stage at the first chord."

Her father wrapped his arm around her shoulders, giving her a squeeze. "Sensational. You were very brave up there, my girl."

"Tell me, Father. Was it you who started the clapping?"

"I'm sorry, my darling. It was not me. It was ... Ah, Your Grace." Sebastian bowed to Nash. "We were just speaking of you."

Seraphina's brow furrowed. "We were?"

Sebastian cleared his throat. "Yes, it was His Grace who began the gleeful cheers for your music."

Seraphina's mouth gaped. "You?"

A slow smile unfurled across Nash's lips. "You seem confused. Does it shock you that a vampire can enjoy good music?"

Seraphina fought against the tingling feeling tugging at her fingertips. "I would say that I find it more shocking that you can appreciate and acknowledge good taste in music."

That earned her a loud laugh from the vain vampire, even though her family's eyes looked like they were about to fall out of their sockets.

"May I offer you a glass of champagne, Lady Halloway?" Nash asked, lifting a sparkling glass of pink, bubbling liquid toward her, showcasing his white velvet sleeves.

She nodded and placed her bag beside her, happily accepting the liquid courage.

"Your Grace, I'd like to thank you again for your generous donations to my family. We are most appreciative," Sebastian said.

"Consider me thanked enough, Sir Sebastian." Nash drew his gaze to Seraphina. "Shall we continue the list of questions I'm supposed to have for you?"

"I suppose you must," Seraphina said with a hint of amusement in her tone. Was she enjoying his presence? No, of course not. How does one enjoy the presence of a velvet vulture?

"Let me see. I believe I should ask what your favorite food is." Before Seraphina could give her rehearsed response, Nash continued, "In which you would answer cherries. I would then ask you what your favorite flower is, and you would say the red rose. I would nod and look surprised by this. After I collect myself from being stunned, I would ask the question of the night: What is your favorite color? And you would say …"

"Blue."

She watched the most powerful man in the room, the preening peacock, freeze at a single word. Her heart pounded with honesty pressing forward, begging to be voiced.

"But not just any blue. The blue before a storm tosses the sea. The blue of a forgotten velvet chair in an old room as the dying light catches its color, fading. The deep aqua of ancient ice pressed below from the ages of time. A blue of promise, a vow wrapped in emotion from unspoken bonds in the shade of the night sky, relenting its final powers over light."

"Dusk," Nash said in a hushed whisper.

The predator and the prey locked eyes, assessing the electricity through those spoken words: rebellion, danger, and passion. A loud crunch interrupted the moment between Nash and Seraphina. She looked down to see a vampire's shoe on top of her fiddle's bag, which was now completely ruined.

CHAPTER THIRTEEN

The Question

This was no accident.

"Oh, my apologies. I hope whatever was in this luggage wasn't important," the female vampire cooed.

Seraphina fought back tears. That fiddle had been a gift from the local tavern. Her brother Simon snuck her there when she was young. She loved listening to the music and watching the neighbors dance and laugh. Soon, the musicians started teaching her how to play. She became one of them, especially when they scraped together their hard-earned coins for a worn-out fiddle just for her.

Now, that sweet gift was destroyed by the formidable stomp of a vampire.

"How dare you!?" Nash snarled.

"Easy, Nashy. We wouldn't want you to develop a soft reputation—would we?" She flicked her sparkling blonde hair and shifted her focus back to Seraphina. "Did you really think your barnyard reel would impress us?" She huffed. "You, my dear, are just a bug sent to entertain—nothing more." She thumped Seraphina's glass, shattering the crystal, and the pink liquid splattered across her white dress.

Nash grabbed the vampire's arm and forcefully pulled her away from the group into another room to avoid prying eyes. Seraphina checked her dress and looked at the broken fiddle inside the bag. Hot tears stung her eyes. She had done her part for the night—her desire now was to leave, ride into the wind, and maybe, if she were lucky, a storm would rage.

"Please, Father, I wish to leave. I cannot stay here in this dress."

Sabastian nodded, and the Halloways slipped out the side exits, leaving behind gossip and hurt feelings. Once Seraphina was hidden inside the carriage, and she felt the horses moving it forward, she burst into tears, mourning the happiness she had just experienced. *Why did anyone have to be so cruel?* She hugged her bag, jagged pieces pressing into her chest and arms, memories shattered.

The carriage came to a sudden stop outside the city gates, bouncing the Halloways around like marbles in a bag. The door swung open, and Nash appeared, like the unnatural abomination he was.

"Lady Halloway, I wish to speak with you for a moment if you will permit me a few seconds of your time?"

Sabastian nodded toward his daughter. Seraphina, irritated that the well-dressed leech wasn't even breathing heavily from his run, took Nash's hand as she climbed out of the carriage, stepping onto the tiny pebbles crunching beneath her shoes. Nash handed her a handkerchief, which she gratefully took and used to dab her tears and dry her splotchy face, eyes puffy.

"Lady Halloway, my deepest apologies for how this evening went."

"Why are you apologizing? You didn't destroy my fiddle nor stain my dress."

"Perhaps not directly, but indirectly I did."

Seraphina folded her arms, trying to hide some of the pink splatters on her white gown, embarrassed to be in such an untidy state in front of *this* vampire.

"Please explain."

Nash adjusted his stance over the stones, boots shining against the new moonlight. "That was Lady Miranda Astroon, Lady Arissa's best friend, and, in my opinion, the meanest vampire in Thornvein Isle. I'm sure she heard of my behavior toward Arissa this afternoon, so she felt the need to avenge her best friend. I'm only glad she didn't take it further."

"Take it *further*? Take it further! See, that's the problem, isn't it—and always will be. She called me a bug because that's honestly what all of us humans are to you vampires. Something weak and easy to squash whenever you want, whenever you're bored."

Nash stepped closer. "No. Don't say things like that."

"Why? Because it's the cruel and harsh truth? Your Grace, I live in the real world, not the posh society that is sugar-coated with the golden delusions of value amongst a higher species."

"Higher species? You know nothing of what you speak."

"No? Then enlighten me, Your Grace. Tell me how humans could possibly be equal to vampires, then tell me how a commoner like me could be equal to someone like you."

Clouds rolled across the sky, casting an eerie glow around the moon. Wolves howled through the trees. The horses moved the carriage several feet away from Nash and Seraphina before the driver finally calmed them down to a stop. Snow began falling on their heads. The scene would nearly seem romantic if it weren't for the scowl carved into stone on Seraphina's face.

Nash took off his coat and held it over Seraphina, stepping even closer. He still smelled like lavender. She reached out for the coat, holding it above her head, then took a step back.

"You don't understand. I am a creature of death and darkness. You are full of life and potential. We are doomed, while you have a freedom we will never know."

Seraphina stood stunned. Snowflakes stuck to the ends of Nash's eyelashes, making the monster look gentle.

"You don't have to be of darkness," Seraphina said.

Nash flashed his fangs in the moon's glow. "See, there you go again ... giving me hope. Hope that after all this time, there's something worth living for."

"What do you mean?"

"Your answer tonight." Nash clasped his hands behind his back and leaned in playfully. "Lady Halloway, it's your turn to ask me a question." He paused and lowered his voice. "Ask me what my favorite time of day is."

Freezing in the snow, Seraphina gathered her courage to follow a vampire's order. "Your Grace, what is your favorite time of day?"

"Dusk," he said, almost not letting her finish.

"Dusk," she repeated.

"Yes, your favorite color."

Her body longed for the shelter and warmth of the carriage, but her heart yearned for answers. "Why? Why dusk?"

"It's when blue begins to fade from the sky, but just barely. It's the only moment when those of the day are still fighting to survive—when the stars and moon begin to reign, and those of the shadows, who don't belong, don't have to hide. But it's also when darkness and light exist together only for fleeting seconds."

Her arms trembled, and she let go of the coat, snowflakes landing on her. She took a step closer, her chest rising and falling deeply.

"You feel like you don't belong?"

Nash lowered his head and swallowed hard. "I am unnatural; a disruption to the balance of nature, forever wishing to be of the light, a thirst that will never be quenched. Dusk is my ballad."

Seraphina laid her gloved hand over her chest. "Oh, Your Grace."

Nash looked up, piercing into her eyes. "But you," he said as he closed the distance between them, snowflakes swirling behind his movements. "You have vexed me with hope." He gently took her hand in his, slowly raising it to his lips, his perfect lips.

Already promised! Seraphina snatched her hand away, remembering yet another one of her secrets.

"You cannot, Your Grace." She didn't want to explain, nor did she want to stand in the snow among a romantic painting she could never have. Instead, she picked up her skirts and ran to the carriage, crawling and slipping inside, not looking back at the vampire still standing in the falling snow, haunted by a missed kiss.

CHAPTER FOURTEEN

The Track

The tarnished clock on the dusty mantel ticked slowly and irritably as Sebastian and Seraphina sat by their fireplace. With the morning light came a note from the marquess, Lord Jared Beaumont, announcing his arrival for an afternoon tea. Seraphina squirmed in her chair, trying not to think about the almost kiss on her hand from Nash.

Last night was the first time she had dreamt of him. He was alone in the forest again. She tried to ride closer, but every stride felt like the ground was stretching further and further away. She saw that his face was broken and in pain, and in her dream, she wanted to fix it.

She had woken up in a sweat, quickly thrown off the blankets, and jumped into a cold bath, eagerly waiting for the dream to fade from her memory, but it haunted her mind and body. Anna arrived in the sitting room with news of Lord Beaumont's arrival. Sebastian and Seraphina stood, ready to greet their guest—well, at least Sebastian was. Seraphina stood out of habit and routine, much like scratching her nose when it itches.

"Good afternoon, Halloways," Lord Beaumont smugly greeted.

Seraphina hated how handsome he was. She wished his looks matched his ugly ego. Then he would perfectly resemble the wart-covered toad he truly was.

Sebastian bowed. "Good afternoon, Lord Beaumont. It's a pleasure to have you here. Isn't it, Seraphina?"

Seraphina gave a short-lived smile. "Of course. It's an honor to have a marquess in our home."

"Oh, no need for that, Miss Halloway," Jared said, sitting on the couch opposite Seraphina.

She nearly corrected him, but remembered Lord Beaumont wasn't present during the festivities, so he wouldn't know about her being called Lady Halloway.

"I returned from travels to Crimsonreach Crossing last night. I must say, I saw more fae there than pirates this time, but business went well. Even had to deal with a few goblins, believe it or not. Nevertheless, I unfortunately won't be able to attend the next two nights of Venom and Vows due to other meetings, but I will attend the ball on the last night." Lord Beaumont took a sandwich from the tray Anna had laid out and bit into it. He swallowed and looked at Seraphina. "So, how has my bride-to-be been doing with the competition?"

"You haven't read the papers?" Seraphina questioned.

"I was much too busy, but I did hear in passing that this year, Lord Nash Everthorne would be attending. Did you catch a glimpse of the legend?"

"Oh, she caught a glimpse—that's for sure," Shiloh said from behind the couch.

"Shiloh!" Seraphina scolded. "What are you doing back there? This is a private call, not for you."

Shiloh scurried out of the room, leaving Jared glaring at Seraphina.

"What did he mean by that?"

"Only that His Grace has enjoyed our family's company," Sebastian tried to ease the tension in the room.

"Your family's or your daughter's company?"

"It's nothing to worry about, Lord Beaumont. My nonconformity merely amused His Grace. A bug for entertainment."

Jared's eye twitched, and he rubbed his hand over his neatly trimmed dark beard. "Of course, but I would advise caution. Vampires are fickle creatures. They have no hearts; they cannot love." He slid to the edge of the couch, elbows on his knees. "Don't feel bad if you don't secure a sponsorship this year, my sweetheart. I will be able to provide a much-improved lifestyle for you, regardless."

Seraphina cringed at his words. She didn't want a life with him, but she had to admit, it felt good knowing she had a safety net if her plan flopped. However, that would only be possible if she failed and didn't get caught. She couldn't rely on a sponsorship from Nash; apparently, he was the fickle type. More importantly, he was unpredictable; too much of a mystery.

"I was able to make a considerable commission with the profits I made selling the Tinsdale family's venom to those greedy goblins. Honestly, it's almost too easy making money at the ports, but the real buzz there was the race, of course," Lord Beaumont said, causing Seraphina to jostle her teacup. Jared's brow furrowed, but he moved on. "Apparently, gentlemen have recruited horses from all across Lurin."

"But that's not fair ..." Seraphina blurted out without realizing she, a lady, would have no need to make such an outburst. Her father and Jared stared at her, both with large question marks plastered across their faces. Seraphina ran through various excuses, but her mouth made no sound. Instead, she sipped her tea, regained her composure, and hoped for the best with her next statement. "I only mean this will hurt your prospects for your rider, will it not, Lord Beaumont?"

Jared's face relaxed, and he smacked his leg. "Not to worry, my darling girl. I, too, have a special breed coming. It will arrive this afternoon, in fact—all the way from the Fae lands."

Seraphina felt her shoulders lower. She wanted to slump into the couch, but she still had to sit through Jared's yapping of this and that. But what did pique her interest was his tactics. He had sent spies to the track because the track was no simple task. The race was never just a few laps around, and then there's a winner. Oh no, vampires weren't so simple.

The track was always laced with magical traps and obstacles—those enchanted to mislead both the rider and the horse. Seraphina's heart pounded as she listened to Jared spill about the deep crevice, blinding fog, icy rocks, levitating waterfall, and, worst of all, giant arachnids. Seraphina thought she was going to be sick.

Vampires were devious.

Vampires were full of tricks.

Vampires were evil.

Every night she had snuck out to train Velamir, but she didn't know how to prepare for such trickery. *How does one fight off spiders and see through fog? Just how deep was this crevice? Could Velamir handle slippery rocks?* They had only dealt with icy stones a few times.

Her hope of saving her family felt so distant, another reason to loathe those pesky vamps. *Elegant parasites! How did they always have the upper hand?* Just once—just once, she wanted to beat them at their own game.

An intriguing idea flooded her mind. *What if she poached Nash for advice on how to win the race?* She had heard his mansion was near the tracks. He must have seen the eerie obstacles, and he wouldn't be surprised by this kind of talk since she already radiated an unladylike aura. But the memory of their last encounter made her spine freeze. She had rejected his kiss. How would he react to her now?

CHAPTER FIFTEEN

The Blood Bender

Seraphina's borrowed carriage stopped at the promenade, the one place anyone of social standing made sure to be during the festivities. It was also the one place that vampires hated to be; something about boring gossip being the only highlight, which served as their excuse, making the allure of exposing the true secrets behind the Venom and Vows rumors all the more tempting for humans.

After receiving Lady Clara Pemberton's invitation, Seraphina scrambled to piece herself together and prepare her tongue, for she was entering a den of snakes. She felt relieved she wouldn't face any vampires, but that didn't mean these ladies wouldn't try to take a bite out of her. If there was one thing aristocratic women had besides wealth, it was judgmental fangs.

Her heels crunched on the tiny cobblestones lining the green park in front of her. She tried to ignore the stares and whispers, but her heart longed to know what was being said. She couldn't help herself. Finally, Seraphina spotted Lady Pemberton, who, of course, looked completely flawless in a pale pink silk dress with a matching hat.

"Good afternoon, Lady Pemberton," Seraphina said with a slight head nod.

Clara completely lost all sense of propriety and squealed. She linked arms with Seraphina, leaning in to whisper, "I am just bursting with news."

Seraphina was quite surprised by the gesture and display that Lady Pemberton had just shown. *Was this how friends behaved?* She felt stiff against Clara's pulls as they walked along the pathway. Could she trust this? She wanted a friend so badly, but Clara was the one who had blindsided her.

"After the other night, apparently Lord Nash went on a blood-drinking bender."

Seraphina's mind went fuzzy. "Wait. What? I ... I don't even know what that is."

Clara chuckled. "Oh, it's similar to when one of our gentlemen has a bad day and tries to drink it off at the club. You do know that vampires have blood bars, right? I mean, the blood is supplied by the black market, not like our giving."

For a moment, Seraphina felt like the stupidest person in the world. She had forgotten that Nash Everthorne drank human plasma, as Seymour liked to call it. Her thoughts and feelings had turned him into almost ... dare she think it ... a human.

"Forgive me. I don't know much about the vampire way of life."

Clara pulled Seraphina closer, stepping in sync with her. "Not to worry. I'll be your teacher. But everyone is talking about Nash's bender because he never goes to vampire bars—never. He gets his supply from that Bloodmist Cove place, or so I hear. Do you have any idea what could have made him lose himself like that?"

Seraphina knew, but she wasn't about to divulge that information. Instead, she shook her head, not trusting herself to tell a convincing lie. The thing she couldn't believe was that her rejection could or would have had such a powerful effect on *the* Lord Nash Everthorne. *Why?* She needed answers.

"Lady Pemberton ..."

Clara patted Seraphina's hand. "Oh, please. Call me Clara now that we're best friends."

Best friends. *Best* friends? *What did that mean, and when did it happen?* Had she been notified and missed the letter? Did people send each other letters offering official statements of this kind of label? She wasn't going to question the Pemberton who had just knighted her with such a title, so she pressed on.

"Clara, why do you think Lord Everthorne went on a bender?"

Clara again gave her addicting giggle. "Surely, you must be joking?" She stopped walking, thankfully under a shaded tree. "Seraphina, Nash obviously has an attachment to you."

"Me? No. I thought ..." She cleared her throat. "No. Vampires ... can't. Right? They—um ... can't, right?"

Clara snorted. "My darling girl, you really have no idea about vampires." She gestured to a bench. "Why don't we sit?"

The two women settled into their seats, both eyeing the others who kept watching them as if they were on stage in a theater. *Vultures.* That's what they resembled to Seraphina.

Clara took Seraphina's hand. "I'm going to tell you what you actually need to know." Clara patted her hand. "So a vampire is cursed."

"Well, I know that," Seraphina interrupted. "They can't die and must survive on human blood. That's no secret."

"That is only *half* the secret of vampires. Their curse is actually pain."

"Pain? I thought they couldn't feel anything."

Clara sighed. "See. There's so much you don't know. A vampire's instincts aren't actually driven by bloodthirst; it's from pain. Pain of guilt. Pain of heartbreak. Pain of loss. Pain of even love."

Seraphina once again felt out of her depth and apparently was being schooled in the knowledge of "actuallys". If she were honest, she would admit she knew nothing of love; only the love one has for her family.

"Love is *painful*?" Seraphina asked with sincere curiosity.

Clara tilted her head. "My dear, have you never been in love?"

Seraphina dropped her head, blushing. "No." She lifted her head quickly. "Have you?"

Clara's smile curved like a secret hidden behind a treasure chest. She nodded her head toward a group of gentlemen a few yards away. "Do you see the tall gentleman with the red beard over there?"

Seraphina looked at the group with the five gentlemen. She noticed the dashingly handsome, red-bearded gentleman wearing a shiny black top hat and what she thought was a pale pink shirt underneath his vest and coat. *Was that the same color Clara was wearing?*

"Yes, I see him. Why?"

Clara sighed a deep sigh. "That's Patrick, and for whatever reason, I find myself madly in love with him. He's shy, where I am outgoing. He loves books, and I love music. He rides horses, and I dance. We couldn't be more opposite, but he's all I dream about."

"Will you marry him?"

Clara's eyes bulged. "Seraphina, that's not really an appropriate question to ask."

Seraphina lifted her eyebrow. "And I'm not really an appropriate lady."

The two ladies fell into a laugh, a real laugh, a laugh of friendship. Seraphina felt this was what friendship truly meant—sharing your deepest secrets and trusting the other person to keep them no matter what. She felt like she had finally found someone like that with Clara. *How strange?* A barrier broken between the rich and the poor. Seraphina never thought a bridge between the two could exist.

Clara cleared her throat. "Well, I do hope so, though. We manage to dance at each ball, and our families do business together, but my father is hard to impress, but ..." Clara's smile sparkled brightly against her ebony skin. "I think this will be the year he proposes."

"How marvelous!" Seraphina said, sincerely excited for her new friend.

"I'm sorry," Clara pressed her laced glove hand to her dark curls. "I went off subject, back to vampires. Knowing that when a vampire begins to develop feelings or affections for a human, they experience pain, and the only way to relieve this pain is by drinking blood. Or, alternatively, killing the human involved. While that might be quicker for them, when draining the life from someone, they endure the most intense, excruciating pain that can last for days or even weeks."

"Is this why vampires made the deal of venom in exchange for blood?"

"Very good. Lucky for us, vampires don't need to drink blood every day. The blood that we do give them is stored in their ice vaults, never wasted." Clara paused, seeing Seraphina's confused expression. "What's the matter?"

"If a vampire feels pain from love or affection, then why not just give in to that urge or feeling?"

Clara's gloved hand covered her mouth, and a gasp escaped. "Because love and marriage between a vampire and a human is forbidden."

"Forbidden by whom?"

Clara's brow furrowed, and her eyes searched the ground for an answer that she didn't find. "Why ... I don't know. It's just always been that way. I never thought to ask why."

Seraphina reflected on her thoughts as Clara exchanged flirtatious glances with Patrick. *If everything Clara said was true, then Nash might have nearly crossed a forbidden line, but it also meant she had caused him pain. Something so painful that he drowned himself in someone's blood.*

CHAPTER SIXTEEN

The Woven Art

Seraphina had hoped to find more answers about her situation during her meeting with Lady Pemberton, but she left the promenade with more questions than she had when she arrived. Her frustrations were frustrated with her frustration. *My, how frustrating.* She couldn't wait for her practice ride with her geminox tonight. That knowledge would keep her going.

She heard the announcement for all the ladies to walk onto the stage, so, like a good little lamb, she followed the herd of women and stood before a pack of predators. Tonight, the ladies were to showcase their talents in art: painting, pottery, or needlework. Seraphina had been dreading this night because it would truly reveal her station.

Her family had no money for paint or brushes, no funds for ovens to bake pottery, and the only needle skill she possessed was patching holes and making clothes, not creating silly pictures.

What a waste of good thread. With special permission, Seraphina would have to create the only other art she knew how—which wasn't even vaguely related to what these ladies grew up learning: basket weaving.

As musicians played in the background, Seraphina wove her birch bark basket using a combination of twining and plaiting techniques her mother taught her. For showmanship, she added dyed porcupine quills to give the basket some extra flair. This was a rare trick she knew how to do, and because of the expense, she usually didn't, but tonight was special. The quills were red, of course—preposterous color.

She arranged the quills in a repeated pattern, only a few rows in the center of the basket. She paused briefly, massaging her hands, and observed the other ladies' work. The competition was fierce. She was very impressed with Clara's watercolors. Feeling weak, Seraphina glanced at the crowd. Her stomach clenched as she saw the first set of eyes … Nash.

He was staring so intently at … not her, but her basket. *Did he look impressed, or was that pity?* She couldn't tell, nor did she have time to think it over. They all had a limited amount of time to accomplish something extraordinary.

She shook her head and refocused on her work, carefully weaving each piece and sliding the handle into place, ensuring it was secure. Seraphina was eager to add her finishing touches. She had gathered green and red seagrass for a striking effect. Binding several green seagrass blades, she began forming the base. After completing the weave, she used another trick her mother had taught her—winding the red seagrass into the green, twisting the woven piece into a perfectly constructed rose shape.

She repeated this several times to create a basket full of red seagrass roses. Seraphina sighed in relief and saw the clock; she still had a few minutes left. Her eyes darted to Nash, then her lips couldn't help but curl into a smile. Nash looked back at her, confused.

Seraphina stood and walked over to Clara.

She whispered, "Clara, do you mind if I use this canister?"

Clara's forehead wrinkled, and she squinted her eyes. "Uh, I guess?" she said with a question. "I'm not using that color anyway. You can use my extra brush right there."

"You're brilliant. Thank you!"

Seraphina quickly grabbed the paint and brush, rushing back to her seat. She picked up more green seagrass, this time avoiding red, as she was worried that the color she wanted might not stand out. Once she had her beautifully woven rose, she dipped the brush into the paint and began painting the rose a scandalous shade. This—this would be her apology.

When she finished, she held up the rose and blew on it, speeding up the drying of the paint. She looked out at Nash, and almost as if they were two friends sharing a secret, Nash smiled. Seraphina felt her heart stop, felt time pause, and believed nothing in this world was more breathtaking than being the reason for joy spreading across that man's face.

CHAPTER SEVENTEEN

The Way to Win

Like a candle in a storm, Seraphina and Nash's moment vanished when Lady Hamilton clapped her hands. Servants rushed onto the stage, carrying the pieces to the ballroom to be displayed. As the protocol states, this evening, the ladies will stand beside their art as guests browse the room. Vampires even took to bidding on the objects, giving the lady the winnings.

Seraphina stood with her hands clasped behind her back in her cotton candy pink satin dress—the same color every lady wore. She snatched a champagne glass from a server's tray and quickly chugged the contents; her stomach was in knots as she waited for Nash. Her mouth went dry as she saw all the other vampires avoiding her basket ... a poor person's talent. Such stupid snobs. She wanted to leave.

But just like after a storm when the clouds part, the crowd did the same for Lord Nash Everthorne as he casually strolled over to Seraphina's display. He wore a fitted black suit with a pink rose that matched her dress. Once again, the pattern of these evenings—apparently, no one wanted to challenge that rule.

Seraphina curtseyed. "Good evening, Your Grace."

"Good evening, Lady Halloway."

"I hope you enjoyed the performances tonight."

Nash tilted his mouth in amusement, part of a game of cat and mouse. "I did, but only one in particular caught my attention."

Seraphina tried not to show emotion. "Oh? And which would that be?"

Why did his essence beg to be flirted with? She had to be careful. She tried not to stare at his golden hair sparkling in the candlelight nor at the way his jaw tightened at the sound of her voice, but her resistance to his *everything* was starting to weaken.

"Why the basket weaver, of course." He pointed at the middle of her piece. "Are those quills from a porcupine?"

"Yes," Seraphina giggled. "I'm surprised you would know that."

"I'm full of surprises, my lady, and it would seem ... so are you." Nash's gaze lingered on the painted rose.

Seraphina gently picked the woven rose from the basket and extended her satin-gloved hand toward the vampire who was staring at her. His sharp jaw clenched, and his eyes flicked from the rose back to Seraphina. After a brief hesitation, Nash reached out and accepted the woven art.

Nash cleared his throat, looking at the gift. "Midnight blue," he said.

Seraphina's lips curled, begging for only his attention. "Dusk, Your Grace. Let's call it dusk."

Nash's head jerked up; his face softened. Seraphina thought she saw a haze over his eyes. *Those couldn't be tears. Vampires couldn't ... but what did she know? Perhaps this creature before her, whom she once thought couldn't feel anything, could feel more than what humans could feel?*

Instantly, she regretted giving him a gift that might cause him pain.

"Your Grace? Are you well?"

Nash quickly snapped out of his trance. "Of course. Well done tonight. You deserve all the recognition possible."

"Thank you. Um ... Your Grace, should we ..." Seraphina bit her lip, not wanting to ask. "Should we discuss last night?"

Nash waved his hand. "No, please. I ... I completely misread the evening, and I hope you accept my sincere apologies. I won't act that way again."

Something inside Seraphina shattered, and sadness overwhelmed her. *What was this? Surely, she wasn't hoping for Nash to kiss her hand? That was ludicrous.*

"Oh ..." She cleared her throat. "Well, now that that's settled." Anger burned inside, and she didn't know why. "Let's discuss something more on topic."

Nash snorted. "And what would you have in mind?"

Seraphina pretended to think. "How about the horse race?"

"The horse race?"

"Yes. I heard it has enchanted obstacles. Is this true?"

Nash's eyes narrowed. "It is."

Seraphina could tell she would have to pry the information out of him.

"So, tell me about them."

Nash flashed a smile with fangs, the kind of expression with a warning. "Certainly." He stepped closer. "A rider must remember these enchanted obstacles are just that—enchanted."

"What does that mean?"

He leaned next to her ear. "They're not real."

Her breath caught, and she repeated the words.

Nash stepped back, studying Seraphina. "That's correct. These enchantments only cloud the rider's and the horse's minds, making them think they see an obstacle."

Seraphina's mind whirled. *How was she to face that and win?*

"Is there a way to win?"

Nash's golden hair creased with his head tilt. "Win? Now, why would a lady such as yourself need to know how to win the horse race?"

She had spoken too much and needed to leave. An idea had come to her, and this new strategy would require a lot of practice. She looked into Nash's eyes, finding kindness. *How strange.* Seraphina never thought she would see that in a vampire, and there went that other strange feeling deep inside her. She would need to have a long talk with herself over these unsettling moods.

Her feelings needed to stay locked away because her situation was desperate. She was promised to another man—a man she didn't love, who would be a frightening husband—and her family's farm was sinking into debt, a debt she could settle if she just won the mind-bending horse race, which would also save her from having to marry the pesky lord. Above all, her feelings for Nash would only cause him pain and bring both a lifetime of misery.

"I meant nothing by it, Your Grace." She studied the room and bit her lip. "Do you think it would be all right if I retire for the evening?"

"You mean leave? Now?"

"Yes. There are some household matters I must tend to tonight."

Nash folded his arms, allowing his front hand to twirl the woven rose. "Sounds more like you're hiding something. Are you a deceiver, Lady Halloway?"

"Deceiver? No. No. I'm not ... I mean, I wouldn't ..." Frustrated, Seraphina propped her hands on her hips and huffed. "I really do have something important to take care of."

With a shadow of a laugh touching his lips, Nash tapped Seraphina's shoulder with the flower, playfully. "Ah, so Lady Halloway does have a secret ..."

"Well, I ..."

"And you don't want to share this secret that seems so urgent to take care of, especially after asking such alluring questions about a particular horse race?"

Now, it was Seraphina's turn to fold her arms. Her eyes narrowed. "What I do with my time is my business. I wish to keep my goings private—not secret."

"Seems to be one in the same. I just hope you know what you're doing."

"What's that supposed to mean?"

Nash dropped his arms and clasped them behind his back. "It means that if your secret is what I think it is, then you're playing a very dangerous game."

His expression darkened, almost making the whole room feel ominous. Seraphina swallowed hard. She knew her life was on the line if she was caught, but she believed the chance of winning outweighed her own life. Her family needed her, and so did her entire future.

"I appreciate your concern, Your Grace, but I can take care of myself. I hope you enjoy the rest of your evening." Seraphina bowed and started to walk away when his hand caught her arm. She looked from his gentle grip to his pleading eyes.

"Won't you stay for the prize announcements?"

Seraphina chuckled. "Forgive me, Your Grace, but I don't need to witness my basket coming in last place. A goblin wouldn't even look twice at my work."

"Goblins are too greedy to know the true value of anything—or anyone."

Seraphina stared in shock at the quick retort, unsure how to reply. Too stunned, she looked away and fidgeted with her hands. With luck finally showing up for her, a loud crash echoed through the ballroom, followed by a scream from a very disappointed lady who had worked hard on her stunning pottery. Seizing the moment as everyone turned toward the commotion, Seraphina slipped away in the opposite direction, heading home for a night full of rule-breaking practice.

CHAPTER EIGHTEEN

The Blinding Light

Velamir's nostrils flared, and white breath burst from each exhale as he pounded his hooves against the icy ground. Seraphina pulled on the reins, gripping the saddle tightly as she rode her trusty geminox blindfolded. Her plan was to keep her eyes closed the entire race and talk Velamir through the enchantments.

It was a terrible plan—possibly one of the worst in history—but she only had days to outsmart ancient magic, avoid getting caught, and win a race she wasn't supposed to. Naturally, bad plans often come from desperate haste.

She smelled the snowy forest, but because she was foolishly blindfolded, she didn't duck as the frosty branch hit her. The hard ground was unforgiving when she landed among the sticks and rocks, scraping her elbow and shoulder. Wincing, she untied the blindfold and threw it, letting out a cry of frustration.

"We've been at this for hours, and I'm no closer to figuring this out!"

Velamir nudged his nose on Seraphina's cheek, a response she took as encouragement. She sat up, noticing her torn clothes, and stroked Velamir's nose and sighed.

"I wish I knew a better way …"

Something snapped in the woods. Bats flew overhead as if they feared what was coming. Seraphina's heart raced. *How far was she from home? No dangerous beasts were supposed to be in these woods, but what if the thing stalking her wasn't a creature—what if it was something worse?*

Velamir let out a nervous sound as the female vampire stepped into the cold moonlight: Arissa. With the look on Arissa's face, no one around to witness, and Seraphina's bleeding wounds, this was possibly the worst situation she could be in. Seraphina sat still, willing herself not to bleed.

"Well. Well. What do we have here?" Arissa smugly asked.

Seraphina's eyes twitched. "I … I was just out riding to clear my head."

Arissa sucked her teeth; a sound Seraphina's spine stiffened to. "Didn't your dead mother teach you not to spin lies to vampires?"

Well, that stoked the vampire-hating fire inside Seraphina. *Who was she to speak to her like that?* How she loathed these emotionless monsters.

"What are you doing out here?" Seraphina almost whispered.

Inching closer, Arissa tilted her head. "The party finally ended, and I wasn't ready to go home, so I decided to walk through the forest. I couldn't help but hear you fall. Of course, I needed to come see for myself just who in the world would be riding at this hour. What a stroke of luck it was you."

Seraphina groaned at the word *luck*. Luck was toying with her.

"How kind of you to check on me, then," Seraphina grunted as she pulled her arm forward, wrapping her skirts around her still bleeding elbow. "But I should return home. I need to take care of my injuries."

"Yes, your injuries ..." Arissa's gaze clouded and fixated on Seraphina's wounds. She took another step forward. "Allow me to assist."

Seraphina could feel Arissa's voracious nature flowing from her; it was almost thick like campfire smoke, yet tempting like the scents of baked honey and cinnamon. Feeling her body's aches and pains, she reached up to grab Velamir's bridle for help.

"No, that won't be necessary ..." Seraphina winced.

It was like living in a dream—the one where running feels endless, screams are silent, and time seems to freeze. Arissa let out a ravenous growl, her fangs aiming for her prey. In those brief moments, Seraphina's hand only managed to grab Velamir's jewel covering, which she ripped off as Arissa yanked her from her sitting position to one now standing, held by a vampire's strength.

Seraphina felt Arissa's sharp fingernails dig into her skin, drawing more blood. Arissa twisted Seraphina's neck at an odd angle, ready to feast on the innocent, but a blinding blue light struck them with such force that it knocked them to the forest ground.

Seraphina wasn't sure how long she had been unconscious, but she awoke coughing and grabbed her head. Her eyesight was blurry, but the blue light was gone; only the moonlight streamed through the trees around them. She sat up quickly, too quickly, feeling several new bruises she had just acquired.

She scanned the area, and Velamir quickly came into focus, waiting patiently for his companion. She felt relieved he hadn't been scared off by the blue light. Then, she looked to her left, and there was a shriveled version of the once-majestic Arissa.

The body was a dull, ashen grey with thousands of wrinkles. Her hair was just a few strands of white, and her face, once considered the epitome of beauty, was sunken and darkened with age. Seraphina gasped in horror. *Was she dead?*

Arissa couldn't be dead, right? Vampires were supposed to be immortal. A wolf echoed a chilling call, signaling it was time for Seraphina to leave. Whether Arissa was dead or not, she wouldn't stay to find out. She fought, scrambling to her feet like a baby deer and somehow managed to climb onto her trusty geminox, but something about her four-legged friend made her think.

Velamir's jewel no longer glowed. *Strange, as it always had. Was there something about geminoxes she didn't understand?* She couldn't dwell on that now. She had to leave this place of the decaying monster because if *that thing* awoke, she wouldn't escape death's claws again.

She kicked Velamir into a swift gallop, the freezing wind kissing her cheeks as the howls of the mountain wolves echoed their final songs of the night. The forest remained silent once Seraphina vanished into the darkness, leaving behind a corpse and a blindfold.

CHAPTER NINETEEN

The Venom

S queals. Sunlight. Headache. Door slamming open. Nausea. This was how Seraphina woke up in her bed. The next thing she felt was her young sister jumping onto that same bed. She thought she was going to be sick.

"Sera! Sera! Wake up! Wake up! You must come see!"

Seraphina moaned in response to the pesky child.

Sophia dropped to her knees, reached out her tiny hands for the covers, and pulled them back, only to scream again, but this time in shock. Seraphina was covered in dried blood, bruises, and torn clothes. She hadn't bothered to clean herself after the night's ordeal.

"Sera ... w-what happened?" Sophia's lip quivered as she spoke, tears welling in her eyes.

Seraphina grunted as she pushed herself upright, leaning against the worn headboard, grateful for her pillows.

"I'm all right. I just fell from Velamir is all. Why all the loud noises this morning?"

Sophia didn't look like she believed her sister, but she answered anyway, "Lord Nash is here!"

"What?" Seraphina's mind spun. *Why was he here? Did he know Arissa was dead? Did he know she was the one who killed her? Wait, did she? No, the blue light wasn't her fault. Where did that even come from?*

"He brought your winnings."

Seraphina's brow furrowed, pained by confusion and dehydration. She was struggling to understand anything her sister said. Her back ached, and her head throbbed.

"Winnings? What winnings?"

Sophia giggled. "From last night. He bid the highest for your basket."

"My basket," she repeated with a whisper.

"Yes. There is a whole bucket of gold coins!"

"What?" Seraphina's vision started to blur. Pain spread from her neck down her spine, then back up through her head. She grasped the front of her forehead, gasping.

Sophia screamed again as blood dripped down Seraphina's nose. Before the younger sister could make another sound, Nash was at Seraphina's doorway, concern evident on his porcelain face.

"Sophia, please leave us," he said in a velvety voice.

Seraphina wiped her nose with her sleeve, scrutinizing the vampire who just sat on her bed—*her bed*! What was going on? Nash removed his leather satchel from across his chest and set it between them. He rummaged through the contents, then paused.

"What happened?" he asked without looking up.

"I fell."

Seraphina felt like the sunny room darkened as she watched the immortal slowly lift his head and glare.

"I did fall. I mean, that's not all, but I really don't want to discuss it."

Nash withdrew her blindfold and tossed it on the bed. "Care to explain?"

This looming mosquito was causing a whole new headache. She felt sick again and inhaled sharply as she tried to move. Nash quickly dug into his satchel again and pulled out a bottle with a silvery liquid. He extended his hand, offering the swirling mixture to Seraphina.

She handled it gently, examining its contents. As the sunlight reflected on it, the silver liquid shimmered with a rainbow of colors. *What was this?* She had never seen a potion like it before.

"What is this?"

"My venom."

Seraphina's heart pounded in her chest as she held the most prized substance known in all of Lurin in her palm. She never thought this would happen, not in her wildest dreams. *Could she really drink it?*

Nash slid closer, cupping his hand against hers in an attempt to guide the bottle closer to her lips.

"Please. Drink. I promise you will feel much better once you do."

With effort, Seraphina lifted the glass container to her mouth and began to drink vampire venom. Although she'd seen that the liquid was thick, it felt like weightless water and tasted as sweet as honey. She felt—odd. Like she was floating in the sea, but she wasn't cold. No, it felt like the first day of summer, sunshine tinting her cheeks and butterflies dancing in the wind.

Her headache dissipated. Her bruises vanished, and her wounds closed as if they had never been there. Even the childhood scar on her palm was gone. She looked into Nash's eyes with a thousand questions.

Nash's lips bloomed into a smile. "Feeling better?"

Seraphina corked the bottle and handed it back. "Yes." She cleared her throat. "Yes, I am. Thank you."

"Good. Now, could you please tell me how Arissa ended up in a petrified state when I found her and your blindfold?"

"How do you know it's mine?"

"Your name is *literally* embroidered on it."

"Oh, that's quite condemning."

Nash chuckled, a sound that made Seraphina's heart skip a beat. She thought she saw him react to it. *Could he hear her heartbeat?*

"You said petrified, so not dead?"

Nash tilted his head. "Dead? You thought Arissa was dead?"

"Since I wasn't there, I'm not going to dignify that with an answer, but I'd guess if someone saw a vampire lying in the forest in a petrified state, would she look dead?"

Nash tilted his head back and let out a deep sigh, then looked back at Seraphina. "I can see we will have to do this the hard way. Technically, all vampires have died—well, the former humans have died, and in their place, immortal vampires have risen, so no, she's not dead." Nash wrapped the satchel across his chest and buckled it shut. "The question is—how did she end up petrified? Because even Arissa doesn't know."

"Wait. She's awake?!" Fear crept down Seraphina's spine and churned her stomach like spoiled milk. *Did Arissa think that she, just a human, had tried to kill her, only to fail and petrify her? If so, what does a vengeful, unpetrified vampire have to lose?*

CHAPTER TWENTY

The Papers

Nash rose from Seraphina's bed and made his way to the doorway. He turned back around, pain written on his forehead. *Was he worried about her? Was her family in danger?*

"Yes, she's awake. As to the petrification, I have my theory, one that stars your secret pet and that jewel you hide." Nash checked his golden pocket watch and cleared his throat. "My apologies, Lady Halloway. I have an appointment I must keep; otherwise, I would stay for the rest of your story, but this is one ..." He trailed off, looking out the window in a trance of the past.

"Your Grace?"

"My apologies, my lady. I will see you tonight, though."

"Care to share about this mysterious meeting?"

Nash propped himself against the doorframe, chin lifting slightly. "I believe I will keep this one to myself."

Seraphina folded her arms. "Now who's keeping secrets?"

Nash mockingly crossed his arms as well. "My lady, I believe we should keep a little mystery between us, and besides ..." He pushed off the doorframe, and in a flash, he was nose to nose with Seraphina. He whispered, "I like you wondering what I'm up to." He winked and, with unnatural speed, vanished.

Warmth spread to her cheeks from his wink. She pressed her hand to her chest, trying to gather her thoughts. Her life was falling apart. Her family was about to lose their home. She was engaged to a scoundrel. She had escaped death from a vampire last night—a vampire who was now likely seeking revenge against her. In three days, she would ride her illegal geminox in a forbidden race that could lead to her execution, but, above all, she was developing feelings for Lord Nash Everthorne, a romance that could only bring pain and heartbreak.

A vampire and a human had no future, so why wasn't her heart cooperating with her logical mind? What a treacherous organ. She huffed and decided that instead of wallowing in her doomed schoolgirl crush, she would check if her sister had been telling the truth about the bucket of gold.

She threw off the covers, and as soon as her feet hit the floor, she stood up without feeling any aches or pains. Seraphina immediately understood why vampire venom was so highly prized. She quickly changed into an old olive green day dress and hurried down the hallways, following her family's voices.

Her mouth dropped open at the sight of the bucket sitting on their wagon with sparkling gold. It was odd to enter her garden and not wish for aid from the heavens ... perhaps this was the answer. Her brothers and father were scooping coins into small pouches while singing familiar tunes.

"What are you doing?"

Seraphina's father beamed. "What does it look like? Paying back those who have helped us in the past."

Seraphina's heart swelled. Of course, her father would think to repay others before settling his land debts. She watched her brothers climb into the wagon and set off to see their debtors, wheels cutting through the snow and mud. Part of her was angry that vampires had all this wealth and never shared it with her people, but the other part was relieved that none of the farmers would go hungry this winter. She could ensure that now.

"Father, with this gold, surely our farm will be saved?"

Sebastian dropped his head. "It will help, but it won't cover all the repairs and upgrades this place needs to sustain itself."

"But the debts—they will be paid?"

"Yes. The debts will be paid."

Seraphina smiled and hugged her father. She leaned back and cupped his unshaved chin. "This means I don't have to marry Lord Beaumont, right?"

Her father's face fell.

"Right?" Seraphina repeated. "Father?" Her voice cracked.

Sebastian flopped himself on an old, weathered bench; her brothers continued loading the wagon, trying not to watch.

"I'm sorry, my darling girl, but you still need to marry him."

"But why?"

"As I said, this gold won't cover our future—your siblings' futures. Lord Jared has more than enough to keep our farm and your family well looked after."

"I don't love him, Father. Please. Please don't make me." Tears began to fall down Seraphina's cheeks.

"I'm sorry, Sera."

"No! I refuse. I refuse to marry someone I can't stand, someone who treats me like I'm property. He wants me to owe him for the rest of my life—I can't live that way."

Sebastian stood, anger and sadness flashing in his aged eyes. "The decision has been made, Seraphina, and you will obey."

Seraphina froze. Something was weighing on his words. She wiped her face and glared.

"What did you do?"

Sebastian placed his hands on his hips. "The marriage papers came this morning."

She gasped. "Tell me you didn't sign them." Her father didn't respond. "Tell me," she cried out. "Papa, please," she wailed like she was five years old again, begging her father to bring her grandmother back to life.

Sebastion slowly walked to his crying daughter and placed his hand on her shoulder. "It's done. I signed them and sent them back with my seal."

Seraphina shoved her father's hand away. "No," she whispered through tears.

"I'm sorry, Seraphina. The only way out is death. You will marry Lord Beaumont."

Seraphina clenched a handful of coins and threw them into the dirt. She took off running at full speed toward the barn. Only Velamir could comfort her now, for a marriage to Jared would be her freedom's death.

CHAPTER TWENTY-ONE

The Debts

Seraphina inhaled the familiar scent of fresh hay and sweet oats as she fed Velamir. A memory floated back to her—Velamir's jewel. Last night, the jewel that usually glowed blue was colorless. *She wondered if it was the same.* Trying not to disturb him while he ate, she loosened his head covering, and to her surprise, the jewel had a faint blue glow, but only in the center.

The entire diamond shape wasn't its usual bright blue, so something was wrong. He looked exhausted, not full of energy like usual. Seraphina tried to relive last night's horrific moments. She paced back and forth in front of Velamir's stall.

Arissa grabbed her.

Arissa stretched her neck.

Arissa went to bite her.

Blue light force, then darkness.

She looked at her geminox's former blue jewel. *Was there more to these geminox creatures than people realized? Could they petrify vampires? If so, how? She feared for her pet more than ever—what if Arissa found out?* She had to protect Velamir.

After he had finished eating, she secured his head covering and patted his nose.

"I think we're both in trouble," she whispered to her four-legged friend.

"Still talking to horses, I see," Simon said.

Seraphina jumped at the sound of her brother's voice. "Goodness, Simon. You scared me."

He laughed. "My apologies. I came to check on you."

Seraphina leaned against the wooden boards. "You didn't have to do that. I'm fine."

"I'm not buying that. Talk to me, Sera."

"Do you ever feel like life has just gotten worse each day since Mother died?"

"Don't do that."

"Don't do what?"

"Blame Mother for everything that's wrong with this world."

"I'm not blaming her!"

"Aren't you? Sera, they were already drowning in debt before she died. The Beaumonts kept lending them money every year and ..."

"What did you say?"

Simon's brow furrowed. "What?"

"Did you say the Beaumonts?"

"Yes. Did you not know that the Beaumonts own the majority of Father's debt?"

Seraphina felt her chest tighten with betrayal. "My fiancé's family is the reason why we're in this mess?"

"Oh, Sera. I'm sorry. I thought you knew. Part of the agreement to marry Jared is to settle the debt."

Seraphina began to pace again, kicking up dust. "This all makes sense now. Father's urgency." She let out a cry of frustration. "I can't believe I didn't see it. I feel so stupid."

Simon moved behind his sister and gently grasped her shoulders. "Don't feel stupid. They hid things well. I overheard a conversation I wasn't supposed to hear once. Father doesn't know I know, but I figured since you were marrying Jared, he would have told you."

"Well, he didn't."

"Here I was trying to comfort you, and I only made things worse."

Seraphina turned to face her brother. "You did nothing wrong. I appreciate you coming after me."

"Let's take your mind off of it." He clapped his hands together and hopped on one of the hay bales for a comfy seat. "What talent are you going to show off tonight?"

Gloom washed over Seraphina. Out of all the nights of Venom and Vows, day four was the one she dreaded most. The ladies had to perform a hidden talent for the bloodthirsty parasites, and the gift couldn't bore them. She had no hidden talents, nor any genius for that matter.

"I had completely forgotten about it, and now, I've run out of time. I don't know what to do."

Seraphina scanned the barn as if the tools and dirt might hold the answers. The siblings then looked up at the rafters, searching for inspiration.

Simon chuckled to himself. "Remember when we used to run across the rafters?"

Seraphina laughed. "Mother always scolded us. She was so scared we would fall."

"You never did. You had impeccable balance, even with your spinning and flipping tricks. That always impressed me."

"Really? Beam twirling impressed you?"

"Yes," Simon laughed. "Too bad that can't be your talent tonight."

Seraphina's chin protruded with a slight tilt. "Why couldn't that be my talent?"

"Uh, first, there are no rafters in the performance hall, and second, are you mad?"

A wicked grin spread across Seraphina's face. "Only a little. I need you to build me a beam to walk across."

"This is a joke, right?"

"No." Seraphina sat in the sand and began to draw her plan. "You'll need to hurry. Use the coins to help get everything you need. I'm sure the farmhands will help. We can do this." Maybe ensuring a vampire sponsorship could even the financial differences between her and Jared, but either way, she wasn't quitting; her siblings' futures depended on her.

Simon, still looking shocked, knelt in the sand anyway, memorizing Seraphina's drawing. "Why not?"

"That's the spirit. You work on this, and I'm going to go work on my costume!"

With a renewed outlook, Seraphina was actually looking forward to tonight's festivities—well, except for the fact that an immortal killing beast might have murder on her agenda for the evening. Aside from that, what could possibly go wrong?

CHAPTER TWENTY-TWO

The Fall

Seraphina adjusted her underskirt pants for the hundredth time, trying to convince herself that this final tug would help her deliver a spectacular performance. Alas, if her nerves didn't stop trembling, all the seams might come apart, but at least that wouldn't bore the insects sitting in those velvet chairs.

So far, the crowd had been entertained with a variety of—sure, talents. From reciting poems to card tricks and even juggling, the flairs were mediocre. Seraphina laughed when a lady boiled an egg—an actual egg. *How did that qualify as aptitude?* That was everyday breakfast for her.

She cringed for her friend, Lady Pemberton, as she arranged flowers in a vase. The arrangement turned out beautifully, but the crowd appeared displeased, offering little applause. Now, it was her turn.

She laced her old ballet slippers tight with bright pink ribbon. She checked all the pins at her hem one more time to prevent her magenta skirt from getting in her way. Yes, this exposed her white pants, but it was the only way to avoid tripping. She would lower the hem after the performance.

Her ears perked up as she listened to Lady Hamilton explain why there was a high beam and ladders in the performance hall. No turning back now. Seraphina stepped onto the stage with gasps echoing at her costume. She smiled and waved, then headed toward the ladder her brother had built for her to climb to the very tall top.

As she climbed, it dawned on her how incredibly reckless this idea actually was. She hadn't danced across beams in years, so why in all the realms did she think this was the perfect time to rekindle an old childhood pastime? She swallowed the bile in her throat; it begged to plummet on the guests.

Once she reached the top, she recalled her memories of Simon, Seymour, and her bouncing from beam to beam, daring each other to do another trick. She pictured her younger siblings sitting on hay bales, clapping as she twisted and turned into a catlike creature.

Before she knew it, her twirls and leaps were earning her applause and cheers. Her confidence grew with each step and each spin, so much so that she decided to finish her show with a series of backflips.

She stretched behind herself and let the momentum of her body pull her legs over her head repeatedly. She felt her speed increasing beyond control. Her foot slipped, missing its target, and she fell. She braced for the hard, marble floor impact, but it did not happen.

Instead, she felt the man's strong arms and chest as he cradled her. She opened her eyes, already knowing who she would see—Nash. He had caught her and saved her once again. For a few long moments, they held each other's gaze until loud applause broke their reverie.

Nash looked around at the crowd, now standing for the woman in his arms. He gently set Seraphina upright, grazing her hand. Seraphina inhaled sharply, cursing her heart for fluttering at his touch.

Doors swung open to the ballroom, grabbing everyone's attention, including the powerful vampire with his arms around a woman he wasn't promised to. As the crowd pressed in, Seraphina felt Nash's touch fade away. She stumbled forward, feeling like a cow being herded.

The dazzling ballroom was filled with tall tables laden with food and drinks, a welcoming sight for Seraphina. All that exercise and spinning had made her ravenous. However, additional tables covered in black velvet were scattered around the vast room, inviting guests and contestants to play cards and other games.

Seraphina didn't know how to play the card gambling games since her family never had the funds to gamble, so she sat at the domino table, waiting for others to join. With adrenaline still flowing through her veins and the thought of Nash's arms cradling her, she didn't notice the vampires filling the chairs near her, so it came as no surprise that she jumped when Arissa, the once petrified vamp, snapped her fingers in front of Seraphina's face.

"Uh, hello? Circus girl, it's your turn to pick seven from the boneyard."

Seraphina blinked, unsure whether she should run, vomit, or maybe draw seven tiles to calm this snappy vampire. She stared at the tiles on the velvet table, scattered around in what was, yes, a boneyard, as the game called this part of dominoes. How fitting for the ironic moment.

With an unsteady hand, Seraphina slid seven tiles toward herself, hoping she wouldn't have to start the game. Before anyone could make their first move, Lord Nash Everthorne lifted one of the male players out of his chair and took his seat, grinning from ear to ear.

"Really, Nash? Did you have to humiliate Nathanial like that?" Arissa questioned with a stern expression.

Nash leaned on his elbows, inhaled deeply, and said, "No." He turned his gaze to Seraphina. "Your performance was spectacular, Lady Halloway."

Seraphina blushed as the other at the table joined Nash's compliments, yet not Arissa, but who's judging?

Arissa scowled. "Yes, bravo. It does take marvelous amounts of talent to fall from a beam."

Nash flashed his fangs, but it didn't stop the vampire to Seraphina's right from playing his highest double, the double six. Nash ignored Arissa's insult and played his six and five piece.

Arissa smirked. "Maybe that was your agenda all along, Lady Halloway."

"What was?" Seraphina asked with genuine bewilderment.

"Why to fall into Nash's arms, of course." She laughed, looking at Nash, while laying a six and a three tile at the crease.

Seraphina cringed. *Why hadn't this bloodsucker remained petrified?* She wondered if Arissa was afraid that she possessed magic. *Why else would she tease instead of accuse?*

Seraphina tilted her head. "I believe you are mistaken, Lady Arissa—that's your dream, not mine."

The vampire next to Seraphina choked on his drink, sending streams of champagne from his nose. Arissa glared at the vampire.

"Jeremiah!" Arissa hissed.

"My apologies, Arissa. I wasn't expecting such a bold statement."

A smile tugged at the corners of Seraphina's lips. She dared to look at Nash, who was beaming with pride. His eyes sparkled. Happily, Seraphina slid her double five piece to connect with Nash's five end. She thought it was a clever move, knowing she didn't want to have high values of points in her dominoes if she lost.

What happened next shocked Seraphina to her core. Steaming with hatred, Arissa reached out, grabbed her champagne glass, drained its contents, then glowered at Seraphina. Arissa looked down, then up at Nash. "You would be correct. It has always been my dream to be his."

CHAPTER
TWENTY-THREE

The Double Zero

Awkward wasn't quite the word Seraphina would use to describe the tension in the air. There was something deeper here; the way Arissa's eyes met Nash's was historic—even miserable. Nash looked like he was in pain, but it didn't stop Jeremiah from playing; he preferred dominoes to drama.

They sat silently, the echoes of ballroom conversations filling their ears, as they played each tile without making eye contact. Seraphina's spirits lifted when she watched Arissa play a two and one piece. This let her play her one and six, a move she hadn't expected to come around.

She wanted to look at Nash, but something inside her burned with jealousy. *Why was she jealous? Nash clearly had many years to choose Arissa, but he hadn't, so what was bothering her?* Then it hit her ... Arissa was immortal; she wasn't. Arissa could have generations of lifetimes to earn his affection, and she never would have a chance—simply because she was a mere human, a poor human at that.

Without realizing all the turns that had occurred, Seraphina noticed that each of them had one remaining piece. Jeremiah slammed his hand on the table, rattling the pieces and shaking their champagne flutes.

"This always happens." Jeremiah threw his hands up. "Go, Nash. I can't."

Nash slowly slid his zero and one tile, connecting it to a five and zero to win the game. Jeremiah wrote down two from his double one tile on the scorecard and motioned for Arissa and Seraphina to reveal their points for Nash.

Arissa turned her tile over and said, "Six."

Seraphina followed the movement, showing a double zero. "Nothing." She finally looked into Nash's eyes, knowing her score held deeper meaning. "I can give His Grace nothing."

Tears welled up in Seraphina's blue eyes as she swallowed the pain of reality. She had to stop living in a fantasy world and face her current situation. She was bound to Lord Beaumont and would always be in his debt if she didn't win that blasted horse race.

She had to take back control of her life and stop toying with vampires and their romance sagas.

She slid her chair back. "If you will excuse me, I must return home. Thank you for a wonderful game."

She hurried out of the mansion into the cold, snowy night air. Seraphina was just a step away from her borrowed carriage when

Nash caught her arm. She faced him with a pleading expression, hoping he would let her go.

"Lady Halloway, please," he choked. "Please let me explain."

"There's nothing to explain. You don't owe me anything, Your Grace."

"But I want to." Nash released Seraphina's arm and brushed back his golden hair, receiving several kisses from falling snowflakes. "With Arissa ... there's a long history with her and her family."

"I could tell."

"But it's not what you think, or maybe it is. I don't want to presume to know your thoughts. I was a vampire before her. My father had me turned against my will, and that's all I will say on the matter. He assumed, though, that I would turn him and my mother, which I didn't." Nash folded his arms and shifted his feet, avoiding Seraphina's gaze. He cleared his throat. "I met Arissa at a ball years and years ago when she was human."

"Human?" Seraphina questioned.

"Yes. Human."

"You turned her?"

"No, not intentionally. My father had many ... *followers*." He winced at the word. "One night, they attacked, killing the majority of local vampires, except for me. They used silver chains and bound me in a cave where they then cut me with wooden knives, draining my blood."

Seraphina covered her mouth with her hand, gasping at the horrifying scene Nash described. She couldn't comprehend how much he had endured—and at the hands of his family.

She reached her hand toward Nash, but he backed away.

"I'm sorry. I …"

"I'm not here for your pity," Nash snapped.

"Hating what you went through isn't pity; it's just wishing I could make it all better."

Nash lowered his arms, and his expression softened. "Oh, my apologies." He cleared his throat again. "My father's followers used my blood to turn everyone into vampires, including Arissa's family. My father wanted to rule over the vampires like a king, but as a dictator. As you can imagine, this didn't sit well with the others."

Seraphina began to shiver. She rubbed her arms, trying to warm them, but it was no good. Nash motioned for her to get into the carriage, and they both climbed in.

"Allow me to accompany you home. I'll continue my tale if you want."

"Of course, please do." Seraphina wrapped the carriage blanket around herself like a cocoon and prepared her heart for more of Nash's story.

"Arissa had apparently persuaded the others to spare me, so she could have me as her mate." Nash raised an eyebrow when Seraphina squirmed, but continued. "They ransacked my home and burned it with my parents chained and staked inside. They thought I would be grateful that they spared me."

Hanging on his every word, Seraphina whispered, "What happened?"

Nash lowered his head. "I have secrets, Lady Halloway. Some secrets I can never share with anyone, so I'll be vague. On that particular night, I had made a very valuable discovery with a goblin named Gibbous and a fae I won't name."

"Gibbous? Wait, wasn't he the original king of the goblins?"

Nash grinned. "You know your history. Impressive."

"I like to read."

"So, yes. Gibbous would be the king of the goblins after our discovery."

"Which I'm guessing you're not going to tell me what that discovery is …"

"Two for two," Nash chuckled, then turned serious. "You see, dear Lady Halloway, the discovery made me powerful—more powerful than any vampire or even vampires combined. With this power and in my rage, I slaughtered Arissa's parents and spared everyone else, even though they fought me and lost. I never trusted Arissa and still can't."

"Is this why all the vampires seem to have an allegiance to you?"

Nash gazed out the window into the snowy night. "I see the way they act, but yes, it would have everything to do with that night. Every so many years, a newly-turned vampire tries to challenge me, and always fails."

"Because of the mysterious discovery?"

"Yes."

Seraphina saw her house growing closer. She didn't want to end their time on such a sour note, but she also needed to close the door on her special connection with Nash. Dash it all! *How was she supposed to do this?*

The carriage stopped, and so did her heart. *What was she supposed to say?* This vampire had just shared the worst night of his life with her, opening up and revealing a vulnerable side—one she could love. But he was still a monster. He killed people—well, vampires. And, they had killed his parents. *Is that how it worked: one parent for another?*

Her mind was foggy, caught between fantasy and reality, struggling to blend the two. All she could give him was the same as that rotten double-zero tile: nothing. She was nothing. She came from nothing, and a vampire's relationship with a human was impossible. *So why did her heart ache?*

"Your Grace ..."

Nash held up a hand. "Don't."

She sucked in a breath, "But ..."

"Lady Halloway, tomorrow night is the final night of Venom and Vows, so I'm hoping you're ready for a night full of dancing."

Nash did an excellent job of changing the subject—much better than she did, but was he leading to something?

"I guess I am. I'm not the best dancer, though."

Nash intertwined his hands on top of his lap. "I want to be forthright with you and be clear with my intentions."

Seraphina thought her heart was going to explode out of her chest. *What could he possibly mean by intentions?*

"I plan to sponsor your family."

Lightheaded, Seraphina wondered if the snowflakes had stopped falling midair. *Had the world come to a halt? Had she forgotten how to breathe? Beat, heart, beat—was it not working?*

"I've never met anyone like you before. Someone who dares to break old traditions, who speaks her mind, who ... who holds my mind captive." Nash slid forward, taking Seraphina's hand in his. "I know my affections are a fantasy, for what can a vampire and a human hope to come from such feelings?"

A tear slipped from Seraphina's eye, rolling down her cheek, revealing her internal pain. How dare her leaking eye give her true feelings away. She opened her mouth to speak, but Nash stopped her.

"Please, Lady Halloway, let me finish or else I might lose my courage." He looked down at their hands as he traced his thumb back and forth over the back of her hand. "I will not ask for your blood, nor blood from your family members."

"What? But you ... you ..."

"I have no need for it." He flicked his eyes to hers. "*What I am* craves another type of blood. As I said before, I have many secrets, and your family would have to be sworn to secrecy."

Stuttering, Seraphina said, "Of course, Your Grace, but there's something you should know."

Nash leaned forward, bracing his hands on either side of her, his lips inches away from hers. "Tell me this isn't one-sided."

"I ..." She closed her eyes and shook her head. "That's not what I was referring to."

"So, you feel something, too?" Nash said with a voice that made Seraphina's heart melt, a voice that yearned for the impossible to be possible, but a voice that was laced with conditions. *What price was she about to pay?*

Seraphina sniffed, blinking back tears. "I can't deny anymore that there's a link—a connection between us that I cannot explain, but Your Grace ..."

Her voice faded into the darkness as she felt his lips kiss her hand. Tingles of electricity rippled through her body; she could no longer deny that this was more than just affection or even a silly schoolgirl crush. Even though Seraphina's entire life had been spent hating and despising the type of creature before her, the feeling of his lips on her hand broke down every brick of her wall of prejudice.

Nash knelt before her, leaning closer—so close she could feel his breath on her cheeks. Her breathing quickened, suddenly no longer feeling the cold, but only the heat from the forbidden romance between the two bodies in the carriage. She wanted to sink into him, but her mind flashed to the marriage document. *If she kissed him, would she be sentenced to death?*

"Your Grace," she said in a whisper, trembling as she watched his glowing eyes fixate on her lips. "I can't ..." was all that could escape her mouth.

"Tell me why. Why shouldn't my lips devour yours?"

"Aren't you in pain?"

"Pain?" Nash tilted his head. "How would you know about my pain?"

Still trying to catch her breath, which had seemed to run off into the night, Seraphina managed to blurt out, "Lady Pemberton told me that a vampire feels unrelenting pain when he ... when he feels ..."

"Ah, I see." Nash caressed the side of Seraphina's arm, making her head spin. "Lady Halloway, I would rather feel the cuts of a thousand blades or the flames of a thousand fires than not have passion for you."

Speechless, she was rendered speechless.

Nash took her hand in his and kissed the top ever so gently. "Here's what I propose to you ..."

CHAPTER TWENTY-FOUR

The Gown

Seraphina woke up the next morning, drowning in last night's revelations, more lost than ever. *How could she feel such a connection to a beast she found horrendous? But he wasn't truly horrible, was he?* Since birth, she had been taught to fear vampires, to see them as emotionless monsters ready to consume humans at any moment. They were her people's masters; that she should be grateful they allowed her to live in their world.

But somehow, all of those teachings vanished the moment Nash made his proposal.

"Be my companion for as long as you live. You and your family will want for nothing. You won't have to succumb to these games nor even look for a husband. Allow me to be your provider, your protector, your friend."

She flopped a pillow over her face and yelled into it, hoping to ease the tension in her aching muscles. After her yelling session, she tossed the pillow aside and sat up, knees pulled to her chest, hugging them, wrapped in her bed blankets. No matter which way she chose, someone else still decided her future. *Was this the fate of every woman here?*

Bursting through her door without knocking, the twins jumped onto Seraphina's bed, both eager to be the first to share the morning's adventures so far.

"Slow down, you two. One at a time. Sophia, you go first, then Shiloh."

Still bouncing, Sophia began, "First, Father already has helpers making repairs on the roofs of the barn and the house. Second, Ms. Hatley set word that she would be arriving in the next hour to take you dress shopping, and three ..."

Shiloh cut in, "There have been several vampires here, asking to be your sponsor!"

Seraphina quickly slid out of bed, hair messy like a rat was running through her strands all night.

"Why would they want me?"

Shiloh stopped bouncing. "Do you really not know?"

"Know what?" Seraphina asked.

The twins snickered, and Sophia answered, "Because you're in the lead! You've won almost every night, Sera. Didn't you realize that?"

Seraphina looked all around her room, reflecting on each night—she thought she had done terribly, but Nash ... Nash had always been the one to reward her with the highest prize. Because of him, she was now the coveted lady of Heedmoor. *How had she not realized this?*

"Oh, and one more thing ..." Sophia began. "Lord Haughtier Than Thou will be arriving soon as well."

Seraphina couldn't help but laugh with her younger siblings at the joke about Lord Jared Beaumont's name and character. She fully agreed. She wished she knew someone who could help undo the marriage contract, but unfortunately, her circle of friends didn't extend beyond their farm.

Anna, their only servant, entered the room, shooing the children out. "Good morning, ma'am. Are you ready to get dressed?"

Why not? Seraphina thought. She would need every second of this day to prepare herself for what she wanted in her life. As Anna dressed her and styled her hair, Seraphina considered a new proposal for Nash. She wanted to race—she and Velamir had trained too hard for far too long to give up now. If she won, her family would be out of the Beaumonts' debt, and maybe, just maybe, she could convince Lord Jared to break the marriage covenant.

She had always sensed that Jared's interest in her went beyond mere curiosity. After her brother revealed that the Beaumonts had been her family's benefactors, or more accurately, the ones still lending money at exorbitant interest rates, she realized that Jared's family aimed to take their farm and its vast land. Marrying her would secure their victory. *Thieving cowards.*

The prize money from the race would ensure her family would never owe those treacherous people another coin, which would let Jared break the contract and find another lady elsewhere.

Many women wanted him, so that wouldn't be difficult. Maybe then, she wouldn't even need to tell Nash about the engagement. She liked that idea.

Once Anna had finished, Seraphina asked for her carriage so she could meet Ms. Hatley, hoping to avoid any run-ins with Lord Haughtier Than Thou. Nash had asked for a sign that only he would understand; one that would declare she felt the same way about him. Then he had disappeared, like the true vampire he was.

She knew exactly what she wanted to do.

Ms. Hatley climbed back into the newly purchased carriage of Seraphina's family. She fidgeted with her hands, avoiding eye contact with Seraphina.

"Please don't worry, Ms. Hatley. I know what I'm doing."

"I wish I could believe you, but Sera ..."

"Trust me. The gown I picked out will be the perfect choice for tonight."

"But going against tradition, Seraphina." Ms. Hatley shook her head. "I'm not sure this will have the outcome you desire."

Seraphina understood the message behind the dress, and it was exactly what she desired. She couldn't tell her neighbor what was really going on because the woman would rush to her father with all the juicy details, just an excuse to talk to him.

After tonight, the entire elite society would know how she felt toward Nash. She repeated his words in her mind:

I would rather feel the cuts of a thousand blades or the flames of a thousand fires than not have passion for you.

She just needed to get her hands on a copy of that blasted marriage contract.

CHAPTER TWENTY-FIVE

The Heedmoor Commons

S eraphina tapped the top of the carriage roof three times, signaling the driver to stop. Ms. Hatley looked perplexed. Seraphina leaned forward and took Ms. Hatley's hand in hers.

"I need to make one more stop. You can wait here."

"But ..." Before Ms. Hatley could finish her protest, Seraphina was already out of the carriage, gazing up at the legendary Heedmoor Commons—the home of society's elite lawyers and those dedicated to marriage licenses.

Seraphina swallowed hard, her mouth feeling cotton-dry. Her palms were clammy, and butterflies fluttered in her stomach. She had to be very careful in how she approached these men since Lord Jared had friends here.

Surely, she could come up with a lie that wouldn't tip him off, but she didn't have much experience dealing with lawyers. She stepped forward and pulled open the dark wooden door.

Aromas of cigars and brandy filled her nose. She choked on a small cough, fighting the urge to run outside for fresh air rather than violate her lungs with such filth.

A younger gentleman stood behind the wooden counter. "Good afternoon. How may I help you?"

Seraphina gave her best lady-like smile. "Good afternoon. I'm here to ..." She paused, realizing she had forgotten to come up with the lie after she had planned to lie. She swallowed, wincing at the dryness of her throat.

"Oh, please. Allow me to give you some water." He quickly filled a glass and handed it to her.

This was all the time she needed to plan her next lines after finishing the glass.

"Thank you. I'm here to review my marriage contract. My father fears he may have signed it incorrectly, and I just want to make sure everything is in order. Should only take a minute to check."

The boy's eyebrows narrowed. "Sure. What name would it be under?"

"Seraphina Halloway."

She watched him browse through several folders, but none seemed to match what he was looking for.

"Could it be under a different name—perhaps your fiancé?"

Her heart sank. She was hoping to avoid this. "Lord Jared Beaumont."

"Oh, my apologies, my lady. I didn't realize who you were. If you would like, I can go fetch Lord Beaumont for you. He's right upstairs in a meeting."

"No," she said too quickly, causing another inquisitive look from the boy. "What I mean is—don't you know better than to interrupt Lord Beaumont from his meetings? He would probably have your job for that." The boy's eyes bulged and began to flip through the folders quickly. "I'm glad you understand."

He pulled out the folder and placed it in front of Seraphina, tapping his finger and nervously glancing around the staircase, as if his mother might come down at any moment to scold him. After only a few seconds of scanning the document, the doorbell chimed, and in walked the last person Seraphina wanted to see—Arissa.

"Now, why would the lady of Venom and Vows be in Heedmoor Commons? In need of a lawyer, Lady Halloway?"

Seraphina jerked her head toward Arissa, not wanting to rise to the bait. "Good day to you, Lady Arissa. My apologies, I don't have time today for chatting. Perhaps tonight at the ball."

Arissa leaned on the counter. "You're really not going to tell me what you're up to? Even after what you did to me last night?"

Seraphina almost forgot that Arissa had revealed her true feelings for Nash, and Nash must have left Arissa to come find her. Dash it all. She kept managing to upset this vampire again and again.

"Look. I'm sorry about what happened; truly, I am. It wasn't my intention to cause harm." Seraphina slid the folder behind herself. "Unfortunately, I'm on a tight schedule today, but we can discuss this more at another time."

Annoyance flared in Arissa's dark eyes. She grabbed the boy's tie and pulled him across the counter.

"Arissa! What are you doing?"

Arissa drew a blade and sliced his wrist, holding it over the glass—all three watched as blood filled the container.

"Arissa, stop! This is madness."

They could hear feet running from above. *Jared. Jared could have heard the commotion.*

"Tell me why you're here!"

"Blackmail? Really, Arissa? Have you lost your humanity so much that you would sink to this level?"

With a loud moan, the boy let out, "Marriage." He panted, sucking in breath as blood flowed too fast. "Researching ..." His eyes closed, and he dropped his head, unresponsive.

"Did you kill him?" Seraphina questioned harshly.

"Ugh. Don't be so dramatic."

With the amount of blood loss, the boy's legs suddenly buckled beneath him, causing him to slump forward helplessly. Arissa lost her footing, slipping on his blood, and the weight of his limp body was not very helpful toward the predator who bit him. At that exact moment, Seraphina recognized the chaos unfolding and seized the opportunity. Without hesitation, she darted out the door, clutching the folder tightly in one hand. Behind her, the room was left in disarray—a bloody scene still fresh on the floor, shadows flickering across the walls, unwilling to keep their secrets. Seraphina counted her blessings with each heartbeat, knowing that blood spilt could have been hers.

CHAPTER TWENTY-SIX

The Preparation

Clouds of dust enveloped them as Seraphina and Ms. Hatley exited the carriage. The driver had made it home in record time when Seraphina shared that a vampire had lost her mind and was hungry for more. Instead of heading inside the house, Seraphina dashed for the stables. She needed time with Velamir.

With urgency, Seraphina saddled Velamir and mounted him. The pair escaped toward their favorite track. The animal's hooves pounded against the familiar path, dodging and weaving through tree limbs and over rocks. It wasn't until after several laps that Seraphina pulled Velamir's reins to stop.

She dismounted and pulled the folder from her pack, strapped to the leather saddle. The creature wandered nearby, eating a rare patch of thick green grass while Seraphina sat on the ground, her back against an old stone wall. She began reading every line in hopes of finding a way out.

The more she read, the clearer it became how binding this contract was. Even if Lord Jared wanted to end it, he couldn't. The only way to terminate the agreement was death. How could that be possible? She read it over and over, only to arrive at the same conclusion each time.

She started to sob. Velamir walked beside her and nudged his nose against her. Seraphina leaned her head on him and stroked his nose.

What if she destroyed the contract? No one would have any record of it. She could hide it until after the race, then, once she had her winnings, she could burn it in front of Jared, freeing him.

A sickening feeling swept over her—what if there was a copy? Seraphina shook her head. This was a risk she had to take; besides, she was out of options. She looked toward the sun. It was time for the dress to be delivered; she needed to hurry home.

To her dismay, her father was waiting for her in the stables. He looked angry, with his arms crossed and a scowl on his face.

"What is the meaning of that dress?"

Seraphina guided Velamir back to his stall, unbuckled the saddle, and gently slid it off. She placed it on the rack, then made sure Velamir's gate was securely latched, still not answering her father. She turned and faced him, examining every inch of his wrinkled face.

"Well," her father said, raising his arms.

"Well, I think it's time to change or else I'll be late, and we wouldn't want that now, would we?"

Seraphina hiked her skirts and darted past her father, who yelled after her, but she didn't look back. No, instead she looked forward, excited for the ball. Something that five days ago she never thought would have been possible.

Like a frantic woman, Seraphina tore off her clothes, jumped into the prepared bath, and scrubbed vigorously, then hurriedly got out of the tub and dried off with a warm, fluffy towel. Anna helped tighten the loathsome corset and tied the layers of petticoats that would shape the skirt of the ballgown.

Seraphina knew most would not be wearing full skirt gowns, but that was part of her message: stand out, stand against the crowd. Of course, the color would already do that, but why not add a little extra sparkle?

Regarding her reflection in the mirror, Seraphina slightly twirled her skirt, noticing the crystals twinkling in the moonlight. Her heart fluttered at the thought of what Nash would think or say when he saw her. She longed to see him smile for her.

How had her feelings turned into a compass pointing toward Lord Nash Everthorne? If she had a thousand guesses, she never would have imagined her hatred for vampires melting all because of one.

For now, she would be content with being his companion, but a small voice told her that someday, she would want more. She ignored that voice and focused on the here and now. She would worry about "the more" later.

Ms. Hatley finished painting her lips a crimson red, then smudged charcoal on her eyelids and lightly brushed rouge over her cheeks. Anna styled Seraphina's long black hair as half up, half down, with several ringlets accented with jeweled combs.

The red cape draped over Seraphina's ballgown, offering warmth and the perfect disguise for what was beneath. She slipped her silk gloves into the red fur muff, concealing their rebellion as well. She noticed the worry on her family's faces as she waved goodbye from the golden carriage.

Tonight, she would secure their future—a long, happy, healthy, and thriving one. Then, tomorrow, she would take back her life. There was no future with Nash unless she severed her ties with Jared.

Death parts us ...

She repeated those words where the contract ended multiple paragraphs. Why did it have to have such a final ending? She understood the seriousness of the actual marriage itself, but the promise before it ... Maybe there should be some leniency?

Her heart skipped several beats as the carriage stopped in front of the mansion's entrance. She composed herself while watching several ladies exit their carriages in red gowns. Some even had red flowers pinned in their hair. Seraphina closed her eyes and let out a long breath.

She could do this. Tonight would mark the beginning of finally achieving everything she always wanted: her family's debts paid off, their protection, and a true companion for life. What more could a girl ask for?

Seraphina stepped into the moonlight toward a new future, not aware of the last-minute visitor to her family's house.

CHAPTER TWENTY-SEVEN
The First Dance

Among the cackling ladies, Seraphina kept her gloves inside the red fur muff, feeling the heat becoming unnecessary since her nerves were warming her with an internal fire. One of the ladies peeked through the cracked-open door and let out a tiny squeal.

"They're all in red, just like the papers said they would be!"

Seraphina wasn't sure who the girl was talking about, but she decided it must be the vampires. Naturally, they would wear crimson suits and dresses; maybe no one would notice if they took a bite then. Seraphina tried not to think bad thoughts about Arissa, but it was becoming increasingly difficult.

Seeing that poor boy fighting for his life while simply doing his job. Seraphina gasped. In the chaos, she forgot that the boy had said two words: marriage and research. What had Arissa done with that knowledge, and what had happened after she left?

She felt her feet shifting backward. She couldn't face this crowd, not when she didn't know what Arissa's next move would be. But Nash ...

With her hands sweating inside the muff, she looked up into a sparkling chandelier and took deep breaths. She thought about Nash's lips on her hand, and then those words:

I would rather feel the cuts of a thousand blades or the flames of a thousand fires than not have passion for you.

She would focus on Nash. Once she set her terms with him, everything would fall into place. She would have freedom. She just needed two more days, and all her dreams could come true.

The door opened, and the ladies walked in wearing shimmering red gowns and gloves. When Seraphina stepped onto the floor, she gazed out at a sea of crimson; it resembled the beginning of a horror novel. As each lady was announced, a vampire would approach and escort her to the dance floor.

And finally, it was Seraphina's turn. A servant walked beside her, ready to take her coat. As Lady Hamilton announced her name, Seraphina handed the warm muff to the servant, then unbuttoned her cape, letting it fall to the floor. The servant froze along with everyone else in the ballroom.

Dusk. The ballgown resembled the sky at dusk, with crystals that twinkled like stars still begging to be seen. She looked out over the sea of crimson gowns and suits and saw the crowd parting for a dark figure approaching. His golden hair draped over his raven-black coat, with part of his hair pulled back, leaving a few strands to frame his face.

His eyes stayed locked on his target, moving gracefully like no one else existed except her. When he finally stood in front of Seraphina, he turned his head to the silent band, who were staring in awe, and said, "Begin." Melodies erupted from the strings and chords as Nash held out his hand to her.

"Will you do me the honor of your first dance, Lady Halloway?"

"With that entrance, how could I say no?"

Not caring that no one else had managed to dance, the two settled into a gentle rhythm, one spin after another, until eventually the rest of the party decided to join. Seraphina noticed her woven flower displayed in his breast pocket, and she smiled.

"Does my dancing amuse you?"

"No, Your Grace, but your suit jacket's decoration does."

A grin swept across Nash's lips. "I aim to please in dancing and decoration."

Seraphina giggled. The laugh surprised her because it felt like relief more than anything. She could be herself around Nash, and what more could anyone want than that?

Nash drew her nearer, leaning in to whisper in her ear. "I have a surprise for you."

"A surprise, Your Grace—for me?"

"Yes, but it's not here. We must travel to my home."

Seraphina faltered in her steps. "Your home, as in leave the party?"

Lips touching her ears, Nash said, "Do you trust me?"

His warm breath sent sensations down her spine, and her hand tightened around his. She pondered the question. Did she trust him? She would be walking into a vampire's house—alone. Just days ago, she would have automatically said no, but now ... now, she wanted to run deep into the dark forest with him and never look back.

With his lips still near her ear, she leaned her cheek against his and gave him her answer, "With my life, Your Grace."

Inconspicuously, Nash spun her closer to an exit door, and through signals passed with eye gazes and twitches, the two slipped out into the snowy darkness, yet they didn't escape a pair of prying eyes that glared, dripping with ravenous hunger and jealousy.

CHAPTER
TWENTY-EIGHT

The Betrayal

The dark carriage stopped in front of Nash's large castle, a sight no human had ever seen except in drawings in the newspapers. Seraphina gawked at the grand structure; its deep purple shingles and black stone walls were shrouded in mystery and secrets. She lost track of how many towers there were and wasn't sure how many floors the castle actually had.

Nash escorted her inside, where a staff of seven other vampires greeted her: his butler, housekeeper, valet, a lady's maid, foot-man, and two maids. Seraphina was stunned by the size of his staff, and she wondered why he had a lady's maid.

"Good evening. Thank you for the warm welcome to my friend. May I introduce, Lady Halloway?"

Seraphina watched as the staff curtseyed and bowed. Their faces showed such happiness toward her that they almost seemed giddy. This was strange. Were they happy about a late-night snack of her, or was something else going on?

"A pleasure to meet you all," Seraphina responded to their kindness.

Nash looked to his butler and asked, "Is it ready?"

"All is as you wished, Your Grace," the butler replied, excitement in his eyes.

Either she was the dumbest girl in the world, walking blindly to her death, or something truly spectacular waited beyond the golden doors Nash led her to. Her heart fluttered at the idea that Nash might have prepared a romantic surprise for her. She had read about private candlelit dinners, rose petal pathways, and written poems of secret love, but when Nash opened the door, none of those things awaited her.

Her heels clacked against the shiny black marble floor, and her mouth stayed open as she looked around the enormous ballroom. Black chandeliers hung from the ceiling, which was painted to resemble a starry night sky. Strings of crystals adorned the chandeliers and were carefully hanging from other parts of the ceiling in perfect harmony with the candlelight, making the entire room appear as if they were floating among the stars.

The polished black marble floor reflected the enchanting lighting, bringing tears to Seraphina's eyes. She realized he had decorated the entire room for her comfort, inspired by what she had shared with him.

"You ... you did all this for me?"

Nash kissed her hand. "I'd do anything for you, but yes, I thought you would find this as a place to truly be yourself."

She couldn't believe he remembered her telling him that she felt like she was truly herself during the night. Riding her trusty geminox without having to explain anything to anyone. Just her and the wind, with the night sky as her witness to true joy. Yet, the gesture of the grand ballroom evoked a feeling in her that she couldn't quite define.

"Oh, Your Grace ..."

Nash scooped her into his arms, holding her as if they were about to dance. He stood with his nose barely grazing hers.

"Here, you will address me as Nash. I am simply a man transcended by a beautiful woman."

Seraphina sucked in a breath, fearing she might not ever breathe again. She felt as if her heart was going to pound out of her chest because it was pounding with a passion for the vampire who held her.

"Nash ..." escaped her lips as she breathed harder, staring at his lips. She felt his chest rising and falling quickly. *Was he as nervous as she was?* Then they were spinning. She hadn't even noticed the music until they were halfway across the dance floor. She caught a glimpse of the musicians, then met Nash's eyes. She never wanted to leave his embrace. His arms felt like home.

As he twirled her and moved to the beats of the familiar songs, they shared laughs, exchanged heated glances, paused intensely, and exchanged gentle caresses. The music flowed into one of the more romantic tunes, intensifying Seraphina's desire for Nash. She paused in his arms as she spun into him, lingering a bit too long. He took her hand and kissed it, letting his chin slide down her skin to her fingers, where he kissed them several times.

He spun her away from him, her body yearning to be close again, to feel his lips on her skin. She quickly twirled back, allowing her body to collide with his. Their fingers intertwined as their feet forgot the steps. Nash brought his head next to hers, turning slightly so his lips could touch her ear.

Their polished bodies, once a majestic facade of discipline and grace, dissolved into vulnerability as they embraced, arms entwined in a silent surrender. Seraphina felt her hands slide through his soft hair as her cheek rested against his. Her knees nearly lost strength as his fingers glided over her lower back. She knew they would have to return to the party soon, and her chest ached at the thought.

She felt his hands gently squeeze her waist, and she slowly pulled back, skin brushing skin until her hand cupped his cheek, and her red lips remained very still in front of his.

A door slammed, and the music stopped. Seraphina dropped her hands. Nash quickly cupped the back of her neck with both hands, causing Seraphina to arch her back and welcome their first shared kiss. She closed her eyes, ready for his lips to claim hers, but then she heard the voice she dreaded the most.

"What is the meaning of this?" Lord Jared Beaumont yelled.

Nash spun around to face Jared, but he wasn't alone. Standing next to him was Arissa, glowing with satisfaction.

Arissa huffed. "Please go on. Don't stop on our account."

"Get out," snarled Nash.

"Well, that would be a no," said Arissa. "I brought someone for you to meet."

"I don't care who that is," Nash snapped.

"Ah, but you should. Shouldn't he, Seraphina?" Arissa said, dripping with distaste.

Nash looked at Seraphina with fear and confusion in his eyes. Tears streamed down her cheeks as she cursed herself for not telling Nash the truth. *But how had Arissa known about Jared? It wasn't public knowledge.*

"Seraphina, who is that man?" Nash asked.

Seraphina sniffed, lip quivering. "He's … he's my … um …" She gasped through tears. "He's …"

"I'm her fiancé!" Jared spat.

The look on Nash's face felt like someone had punched Seraphina in the stomach. She had hurt him. *How could this happen?* She reached out her arm toward Nash, but he stepped away.

Reveling in everyone's chaos, Arissa stepped forward with documents in her hands. "I found these hidden in Seraphina's room."

"And what would those be?" Nash snarled.

"They're the signed marriage contract between Lord Jared Beaumont and the lovely Lady Seraphina Halloway. Now, why this woman had this file in her possession is beyond my knowledge and probably a good question for Lord Jared, but I, for one, am most curious why the innocent Seraphina didn't share her happy news with you, Nash."

Nash stared at the floor, not speaking.

"Nash, please …" Seraphina said, attempting to touch his arm.

Nash snatched his arm away, stepping further toward the door. "Get out."

"What?" Seraphina whispered.

"Get out! All of you, get out!" Nash roared, and with his unnatural speed, he vanished from the dazzling ballroom.

Seraphina let out a cry. She picked up her skirts and ran outside, receiving the cold, bitter night air.

"Seraphina! Seraphina, wait!" Jared called after her. He took a deep breath as he and Arissa stood behind Seraphina, their shadows cast on her by the castle light. "How could you do this to me?"

Seraphina turned to face the two menaces. "How could I? You and my father cooked up this entire marriage without my consent."

"That is enough, you ungrateful peasant. For this embarrassment, you will never know a moment's happiness for the rest of your life." He stepped forward, pointing his finger at Seraphina. "You will be my wife in name only, and I will not clear your family's debt. In fact, I will evict them and hire them as my servants for less than any low-life out there."

"No, please. Please don't take this out on my family."

Jared made a condescending snort. "I don't want to hear another word out of you. Get in the carriage. I'll take you home, and we'll not speak of this night ever again." He stood face to face with Seraphina. "But oh, how you'll always remember it."

He stomped past her and got into the carriage. Seraphina wiped her cheeks, glancing back at the castle and hoping the dark figure behind the top window would come down and save her from her fate.

Arissa cleared her throat, a strange and new expression adorning her face. "Oh, Seraphina. I didn't know."

Seraphina held up her hand. "Stop. No. You've done enough. You wanted my heart as broken as yours, and you've succeeded, so congratulations."

CHAPTER TWENTY-NINE

The Family Fight

Seraphina sat quietly at breakfast while the family looked around awkwardly, now accustomed to being showered with presents and prizes from Seraphina's winnings. No packages had arrived, not even a single rose or letter. Seraphina tried not to care, but a sharp ache radiated deep inside her.

She focused on her brother reading the paper's predictions about who would win today's race. The race had been her true prize anyway. If she were honest with herself, she wanted to race regardless of her circumstances. The thrill of it was too enticing. Her mother used to tell Seraphina that her adventurous side would be the death of her—one day.

But Seraphina needed to be serious; truly, her future's happiness relied on that race, too. She grabbed more eggs, bacon, and toast, for she would need all the strength she could get from this breakfast to beat the professionals she would face.

Anna poured another cup of coffee for Seraphina, and she stirred in way too many sugar cubes to consider the drink as liquid anymore.

"Are you all right, Seraphina?" her father asked.

"Of course, Father. Why do you ask?"

"Well, I've never seen you drink sugar, and your appetite is quite large this morning."

"It's marvelous how observant you are over my breakfast habits, but you simply lack the eyes to see the more important matters."

The table froze. Simon swallowed his mouthful of eggs, while Shiloh choked on his juice, sending orange liquid out of his nose. Sebastian threw his napkin on his plate, making his fork and knife clink.

"Exactly what does that mean?" Sebastian asked through gritted teeth.

Seraphina stood, chair scraping against the cold, stone floor. "It means that my entire existence is only to satisfy your debts, no matter the costs."

"Costs?" Seymour questioned.

Seraphina snapped her head to her non-empathetic brother. "Yes, Seymour. Costs." She faced her father. "I will be subjected to a life of misery because Lord Jared Beaumont is a monster, devoid of any humanity."

Sebastian pointed his finger at his defiant daughter. "Now, wait just a minute. Lord Jared has always been kind to me."

Seraphina waved her hand dismissively. "Oh, jump off it, Father. He's not present to hear your honey praises, but he did declare last night that I will be miserable in our marriage, so there. I hope you're happy, Father, because it's a guarantee that I won't be."

She whirled around and ran out to the barn, clouds of white bursting from her lips with each breath. Pain clenched her chest. She hated arguing with her father and honestly didn't want to blame him for everything. After all, Jared's tongue-lashing came because she had been caught alone at Nash's house.

She kicked at the dirt, wishing it would satisfy her stress, but all she could do was keep replaying Nash's face of betrayal again and again. *Why couldn't she have just been honest with him from the start?*

Unlocking Velamir's stable, Seraphina gently slid the bridle onto his head and led him out. Her only chance at happiness now was the race... and hadn't that been her plan all along? Yes, she would win this race and reclaim her life.

She finished saddling her geminox in a daze, unsure of what fate awaited her. Tears kept her cheeks glistening with her brokenness. She rested her head against Velamir's, softly petting his nose.

"Seraphina?" a small voice said.

"Yes?" She looked around her large steed and saw young Sophia standing in the barn with tears in her eyes. "Oh, Sophia. Don't cry." Seraphina knelt before her little sister, wiping her wet cheeks.

"But I don't want you to be unhappy. I don't want that mean man to mistreat you, and I don't want you and Father to fight."

Seraphina hugged the small child, then pulled back to look into her big, innocent eyes.

"One day, when you're much older, you'll understand. But for now, I want you to know that I love our father very much, even if we don't always agree. As for the almighty Jared, I might have a plan, but it's not a guarantee. Will you help me?"

Sophia nodded her head fast.

"Good. I have somewhere I need to be, so if anyone comes around the house looking for me, I need you to say that I've gone to Crimsonreach Crossing."

"The southern port? But why?"

"Why isn't important. I need you to remember that. Can you promise to say those exact words for me?"

Sophia hesitated. "Uh, yes. I can do that."

"Excellent."

Seraphina stepped back and faced Velamir's saddle. She lifted her foot and carefully placed it in the stirrup, then gave herself a strong jump from her right leg, swinging it over the saddle. Her eyes caught her sister's confusion, as she was not riding like a proper lady.

"Remember, Sophia. Only those exact words. Nothing else."

Sophia nodded.

Seraphina gently nudged Velamir to move forward but pulled on the reins. She looked down at her sister. "I love you, Sophia." Then she kicked Velamir hard, and they raced out of the barn, leaving a small child alone, yelling out, "I love you too!"

CHAPTER THIRTY

The Race

After changing into her disguise at the ruins, Seraphina rode into vampire territory where the race would take place. The crowd was larger than she had expected. Anxiety crept over her, knowing that even one mistake could cost her her life, and probably Velamir's as well.

Seraphina dismounted her creature, holding the reins in her hand, with Velamir following her. She leaned over the sign-in station to receive her badge. Her group would be the last. Each wave consisted of ten riders, with ten waves in total. One hundred competitors, all with one goal in mind—gold.

That gold represented her freedom, her family's health, and her independence. She could almost taste it. While waiting in the designated area for the competitors, she heard the cheers of the crowd, the screams of panic from the riders, and the neighing of fear from the horses. Bile crept up her throat like a vine twisting around a tree.

All too soon, she heard her group being called. She mounted Velamir with trembling hands, checking one last time that her blindfold was still in her pocket. They had to achieve the fastest time. Two laps. It was a very short race in terms of horse races, but those enchantments made it feel like an eternity.

She trotted up to the starting line, pulled on the reins, and waited for the gun to sound. Her heart pounded so loudly it was impossible for her to hear the people in the stands. She couldn't help but gaze at the faceless crowd and hope she would see … Nash! Nash was here.

She squinted and felt like he was staring directly at her. *Would he reveal her secret?* He could, and he would be justified in doing so. This was the perfect moment for him to take his revenge, but instead, she saw him give a slight nod. *Surely, he wasn't cheering for her, was he?*

Bang!

The gun fired, and hooves thundered across the ground. She quickly reached into her pocket with one hand and pulled the pre-knotted blindfold over her eyes. The first obstacle was the large chasm.

"Okay, Velamir. Remember, you will see a hole, but it's not real. Please understand me. It's not real."

She repeated the words religiously, listening to the horses in front of her screech out in protest. She heard riders fall from their mounts during the protests, followed by other loud landings as horses jumped over the enchantment.

"This is it, Velamir. You can do this. It's not real."

She waited for the jump, but it never happened. He kept running fast, passing others as she heard the horses. *What was going on? Had he gone around it?* Her questions were quickly cut off by screams of terror: giant arachnids. Her stomach clenched.

"Those monsters aren't there, Velamir. It's only a trick."

She waited for her geminox to react upon seeing such monstrous creatures, but he made no such movement. A sudden jerk almost made her fall from the saddle as Velamir avoided bucking stallions and rolling riders. After dodging the chaos, he simply pounded away as if this were their usual training routine. Seraphina couldn't understand what was unfolding. She could hear only two or three other riders ahead of her. Her hesitation at the start came from seeing Nash, which had compromised their position, but Velamir was recovering quickly and unnaturally.

Next was the floating waterfall, but she felt nothing, and Velamir didn't slow down. She expected him to stumble over the icy rocks as she heard the leaders slow and give confusing commands, but her geminox never lost speed. He took the lead.

Seraphina's heart leapt when she realized no one was in front of her. They could win. Her goal was truly within reach. She was so proud of Velamir, even the final enchantment didn't slow him down. His hooves kept pounding into the ground, securing Seraphina's mission.

Questions lingered in her mind, and past experiences surfaced as she rode. Velamir had been present when Arissa was petrified. Velamir showed no reactions to any enchantments. *Could his partial unicorn bloodline have granted him magical gifts and abilities?* This seemed logical. Geminoxes had to be immune to enchantments, and one of their powers might be to petrify vampires. *Was this the reason the law condemned their existence?*

Oh, how she wanted to hug Velamir. She had no idea how extraordinary her sweet pet was when she found the poor baby trapped. All she wanted was to protect and love him, and she did. She had given him a wonderful life with her and her family.

She knew that with Velamir's resistance to the enchantments, they would finish the fastest—they would win. Her heart soared with this revelation. She would be free. All her family's debts would be paid, and she wouldn't have to marry Jared. Happy tears soaked her blindfold as she listened to his pounding hooves.

Once he crossed the finish line, Seraphina heard the announcer stutter through his words: "Uh, well. There's obviously no doubt who the winner is. Sir Halloway riding Velamir!"

Seraphina expected the crowd to cheer for their record-breaking time, but clearly, from their silence, they were not impressed. She quickly lowered her blindfold and saw the scowling faces. She dismounted and petted Velamir, congratulating him on an excellent race.

The two were led to the winner's circle, where the crowd gathered, ignoring the echoing screams of the still-racing contestants. Seraphina beamed as a race official draped a garland of red roses around Velamir's neck. Small applause rippled through the onlookers.

The announcer stood close to Seraphina and, using his projecting voice, boomed, "Congratulations to you both. Please, tell us how you managed such a fast time?"

Seraphina grunted and tried to sound manly. "Used a blindfold, so I saw nothing."

A man in the front was pushed aside, and there appeared Lord Jared, who was carrying a very smug expression.

"And your horse? I didn't see him wearing a blindfold, or perhaps that head covering is against the rules? Sir, remove it," Jared cried out over the noise.

CHAPTER THIRTY-ONE

The Death

Seraphina froze. If they took off Velamir's head covering, everyone would see he was a geminox, and he'd be executed. How could she protect him? What should she do?

"No. My horse just isn't scared like all the others. He's a trained war horse."

There. That should do it, she hoped. But the look on Jared's face said otherwise. Her eyes pleaded with the crowd to leave Velamir alone, but Jared had a large bet on his horse, so she knew he wouldn't let this issue go.

"I said—remove it! If there's nothing to it, then it won't matter." He turned to the people. "Right? Let me hear you if you think I'm right."

The crowd erupted in agreement. Seraphina moaned. She wasn't sure how many vampires Velamir could petrify at once, but they could outrun these people; she would have to act quickly. As soon as she started to turn to mount her steed, Arissa grabbed her arm.

"Rules are rules, sir."

With the blink of an eye, Arissa ripped off Velamir's head covering, revealing his blue diamond gem in the center of his head. The crowd gasped and pointed.

"It's a geminox!"

"He's a cheat!"

"Kill it! Kill them both!"

A lump formed in Seraphina's throat. Just minutes ago, she had felt like all her dreams were about to come true, and now, everything was shattered. Before Seraphina could defend her beloved Velamir, she felt her face covering and hat pulled from her head violently. She stared at the stunned expression on Arissa's face.

Again, this vampire had betrayed her.

"Seraphina," Arissa gasped. "I didn't know."

"Seize her! Take them both to the criminal courtyard!" someone yelled.

The reality of her nightmare coming true hit Seraphina hard, and she started to panic, tears sliding down her rose-colored cheeks. As her arms were tied behind her, she watched in horror as people seized Velamir's reins, pulling him toward the center of the criminal platform. *He was innocent; his only crime was being born. Why would they do this?*

She fought against her bindings in vain; her black hair falling around her face and shoulders. Her throat filled with vomit as she tried to force it back down. She scanned the crowd, not wanting to see her family witness her final moments. *How could she not have thought about them with this possible ending?*

This would ruin them. It would break her father. Her last words to him were spoken in anger. She needed to make amends. Pulling against the restraints, she yelled in frustration. She glanced at Velamir, whose eyes looked confused and scared. Her heart broke. This life was so cruel and unfair.

"By order of decree, no geminox is allowed to live past birth. This creature is an abomination to mankind and all creatures alike."

Seraphina screamed her protests, "No, they're not! They're innocent!"

The crowd shouted their distaste back.

"Also, by order of decree, no female shall participate in the Venom and Vows horse race. If found doing so, the punishment is death with no trial."

Gasps and whispers echoed around Seraphina.

"What we will all witness today are actions not by our doing, but by this selfish girl. She aided this geminox, chose to disguise not only it but herself, and ride in a forbidden race for her gender, and for what? Money! She is greedy and selfish, and today, we will watch her punishment for such things," the chairman of the race said. "I am bound by the law, and the law cannot be undone once it has been broken."

Seraphina looked at Velamir with red, swollen eyes and felt relief, knowing her grief over his loss would be brief since her own death would come soon after.

"Stop!" a voice yelled across the vast sea of people.

Seraphina eyed the parting crowd, breath catching as she watched Nash float through like it was a typical Tuesday.

"Your Grace," the chairman said with adoration. "With respect, you know I cannot release them."

"I understand, and I respect the law, which also states that if someone takes responsibility for one of the criminals charged in the same crime, then one life can be spared, correct?"

Seraphina began to shake her head, realizing what Nash was about to do. He was going to sacrifice Velamir so she could live. She didn't want that. His sacrifice would still be wrong.

The chairman fumbled over his words, "Uh, well, yes, Your Grace. That is correct."

Nash turned to face Seraphina, pleased with himself. "Good. Because I take full responsibility for the geminox, he will be banished from human lands and reside on my estate for his remaining years."

The crowd gasped. Seraphina's mouth dropped. She couldn't understand. Although she was relieved for Velamir, she was hurt. Was he this angry with her for not telling him about the forced engagement? Her head was spinning, and her heart was breaking all over again. *How many times could one's heart break?*

Her heart had chosen Nash without her permission. Years of prejudice finally melted, and she was finally ready to devote all her affections to him and him alone. But his coldness felt like a dagger deeply embedded, a sharp, agonizing pain she wouldn't wish on anyone, even Arissa. Could he not see her remorse? He could steal her away and they could live in hiding, but what a selfish desire that would be. Resolving, Seraphina decided to surrender to whatever fate Nash chose for her human life, because what is love without trust? She would leap off the cliff of faith, hoping wings of passion would carry her back to his arms, as she longed to be his companion for life.

"And the girl?" the chairman asked.

Nash moved closer to Seraphina. She could smell his scent of sandalwood and fresh pine, with a hint of that blasted lavender. Her lip quivered as he looked into her eyes, wishing for a different life. She silently pleaded for mercy.

"The law is the law. Lady Halloway must die."

Seraphina's lips parted. *What could she do?* There was nothing. She had broken the law and had to face the consequences. She even knew this might happen, yet she still went ahead—ultimately, she was a criminal.

The chairman bowed. "At once, Your Grace."

Nash raised his hand. "No, I will be the one to do it."

Seraphina's brow furrowed, and her blue eyes brimmed with tears. She didn't want to process what he said. Panic set in.

"Nash," she whispered. "I'm sorry. I didn't mean to keep anything from ..." She gasped for air, trying to get out the words she desperately needed to tell him. "I—I love you."

Nash stepped almost nose to nose with her, pressing his finger to her lips. "Shhhh. I know everything."

"How?" she whispered.

"We don't have time, but I had a long discussion with Ms. Hatley." His tone was full of compassion and understanding, almost giving Seraphina a moment of hope.

Of all the people in Heedmoor, Ms. Hatley would be the one person to know all her family's secrets. She wished she could wrap herself in one of Ms. Hatley's tight hugs one last time.

Like the kiss of a whisper, Nash slipped a bottle with sparkling red liquid swirling inside into her hand. "This is the secret to becoming a vampire like me. It's a mixture of my blood, fae blood, and white goblin crystals."

"But I thought ..."

"You need my blood and venom to become a vampire, but I've spent my life becoming a different breed, which is where the fae and goblins come in. One cannot simply ingest the essence of a vampire; my venom must be injected into your veins."

Seraphina shook her head. "What are you saying, Nash?"

"I'm saying." Nash slipped off the ropes, binding Seraphina's hands; one clasping the bottle, while he held the other. "Let me give you death, so you can live a life with me."

A smile tugged at the corners of Seraphina's lips. A loophole. Nash had discovered a way to obey the law and for them to be together.

She popped the cork and downed the liquid that burned her throat. "Take my life, and if you'll have me in death, I'll be yours forever."

Nash flashed his fangs, but before releasing them into her skin, he gently kissed Seraphina's lips.

The crowd gasped, not expecting the illegal romance before them. *Such judgy little dandies.*

"Ready?" Nash asked.

"Ready ..."

Seraphina inhaled softly, tilting her head back gracefully and offering Nash unobstructed access to her delicate, porcelain-skinned neck. Her breathing was rapid, and her eyes shimmered with anticipation and trust. She forgot about the crowd;

it was only Nash and her. Everything else faded away into the distant clouds.

Like a creature of the night, Lord Nash Everthorne sank his fangs deeply into Seraphina's neck, draining her human life away. Seraphina went limp in his strong arms, and when he pulled back, Lady Halloway was dead.

Two small trails of blood dripped from the puncture wounds on her neck. Nash scooped her into his arms and walked to his carriage; his servant followed with Velamir. Once Nash was inside his home, he took Seraphina's body to the lady of the house's bedroom and laid her on the giant bed.

Nash clung to Seraphina's icy, lifeless hand, waiting for his love to return. Hours passed in silence, the wind's mournful wail echoing around them, until at last, her finger stirred, and softly, her lips parted.

EPILOGUE

TWO YEARS LATER

A twig snapped, causing her head to jerk. He was near-by. Her heart thumped rapidly, bracing for what might happen next. She suddenly broke into a run—faster than the wind through the trees, faster than a hummingbird's wings. She moved with an unnatural force—a creature born of darkness, yet created by love.

For a moment, she thought she had outrun him, but she paused, shoes digging into the icy forest ground at the sudden stop. There he was, standing in front of her, fog swirling around the dark, massive figure.

His eyes glowed at the sight of her, signaling he was hungry, but Seraphina wouldn't give up so easily. She darted sideways, but he caught her. She tilted her head upward to look into the eyes of a beast—the eyes of the man who had ended her life.

"Will you ever tire of this game?" he asked.

"Why, are you out of breath?" she jeered, knowing vampires don't technically breathe.

He snorted. "Never. But I would like to spend some of our honeymoon not running."

Seraphina wrapped her arms around Nash's neck, fingers running through his golden hair. She felt his hands slide from her back to her waist, causing her knees to weaken. Her lips met his, craving more. She didn't realize how deeply she could love someone else.

She leaned back and stroked his cheek. "Something like that, Your Grace?"

Nash smiled, flashing his fangs, and chuckled. "Something exactly like that ... Your Grace." Nash deeply inhaled near her neck. "You are still the best-smelling creature."

Seraphina couldn't help but smile tenderly at the memory of meeting Nash for the very first time, dressed as a male rider, her mother's lavender soap subtly revealing her. She had looked so innocent then, but now, her lingering lavender scent would stir her husband's deepest passions.

Nash winked. "However, we must get back to the house. Remember, your family is coming for dinner tonight."

"I completely forgot."

"Honeymooning for a month will do that. Your father left a note saying he'll be bringing your neighbor as his ... date." Nash wiggled his eyebrows. "Perhaps, we could host their wedding at our estate."

"My father would have to muster the courage to ask her first."

Nash twirled his bride as they fell into the rhythm of the forest song. "Well, if I know the twins, they're probably plotting something."

They laughed, knowing that was exactly who Sophia and Shiloh were, as they danced under the snowy branches.

Seraphina breathed deeply, drinking in Nash's scent. "I also had a letter from Seymour this morning."

"Good news, I hope."

Seraphina nodded. "Very good news. He's receiving the highest marks at Heedmoor College, and he said that Simon will be returning from the Fae realm in time for the festival next month."

"And ..."

"And? How did you know there was an 'and?'"

Nash chuckled with victory on his face. "Because I have eyes everywhere."

"Fine. He may have mentioned that Simon met someone there and wants to bring her to Heedmoor to meet us!" Seraphina paused and narrowed her eyes. "But you knew that too, didn't you?"

Nash spun Seraphina, then dipped her. "Do you have to ask?"

"Nothing shocks me anymore," Seraphina said as Nash lifted her up and stroked her cheek. "Well, that's not true. I am still in shock that Lady Hamilton wanted me to host and be head of the Venom and Vows committee."

Nash stopped dancing and folded his hands behind his back. "Well, you're a powerful vampire now. One with actual experience of being a contestant and a sponsor, so you're the perfect choice as leader."

"I have several ideas. They might shock a few, though."

"I would expect nothing less from you. I'm assuming you saw the newspaper headlines with today's mail?"

An evil grin swept across Seraphina's lips. "Oh, you mean the part updating the world about dear sweet Arissa mucking out geminox stables?"

Nash shook his head and snorted. "That would be the one."

"I might have read it several times." Seraphina flashed her fangs.

"I'm sure you did. That was an inventive punishment! Oh, and your former fiancé sent us a wedding invitation."

"You're joking."

Nash sighed. "I expect nothing less from someone like that, but the invitation fit nicely in the flames of the fireplace."

Seraphina lost herself in laughter—in the joy of her life—in the presence of the man, the creature she loved. With snowflakes falling around them, she leaned her head on Nash's chest, holding his shoulder. "Nash, thank you for saving my life, and Velamir's."

Nash took Seraphina's hand and kissed it. "The pleasure was all mine."

Seraphina giggled. "Who knew?" she leaned her head back and looked deep into her vampire husband's eyes.

"Knew what?"

"Who knew that in death, there is life ..."

AND THEY LIVED *eternally* EVER AFTER

About The Author

MAEGWEN SALLEY-MASSIE is the author of The Emerald Queen Series, and her story "Creek Rat Jax" is featured in the anthology Riptide. She grew up in the Pee Dee Low Country of South Carolina with her loving parents and sister. Her childhood was spent mainly outdoors: building forts, riding horses, playing capture the flag, riding ATVs, and playing volleyball.

She is a woven polypropylene specialist by day, COO of 963 Film Group, COO of Green Ferns Publishing House, owner of The Well, and a fantasy fiction author by night. Her favorite food is sushi, and she loves to travel the world. Maegwen currently lives in Myrtle Beach, S.C., with her husband, Kyle, their cat, Khaleesi, and their Australian Shepherd, Pogue.

N
W E
S
LURIN
THORNVEIL ISLE
AKININIA
NEBRARIA
BOER
LUMIARA MOUNTAINS
ROSEMERE
OCEANEA
SANDOVAL
EKLOS

Other Books in the Series

Acknowledgements

I always like to give credit where credit is due, so let us begin, shall we?

This book series came about because author Courtney Denelsbeck had a dream of writing a mermaid book in a multi-author series featuring clean fantasy stories. Thank you, Courtney, for having the courage to ask the question on Threads.

When writing, an author always faces walls of blank—endless spaces of pure nothingness that add no value to life, or the white pages with the bothersome blinking cursor. So, who did I turn to for rescue? That would be C.A. Meadows and Sofia Simpson. Thank you, ladies, for your fantastic banter and for being willing to bounce ideas off one another.

A book is always judged by its cover; c'mon, you know you do that. I want to make sure to give Candice Pedraza Yamnitz the magnificent credit for creating all our book covers in this series. Well done, Candice, and thank you for your hard work and time.

Let me say that I had more beta readers for this book than any other book I've written—I think people really like vampires or something. Allow me to list the splendid beta readers because

I truly appreciate each one's efforts, critiques, and encouragement:

Lydia Hancock, Linda Gleason, Gwen Williams, Brooke Baucom, Wendi Vicari, C.A. Meadows, Courtney Denelsbeck, Caitlin Wolfe, Deirdre Hardwick, Kim Guerini, Vee (@EscapingInPages), Sofia Simpson, and Nora Smith.

To my lifetime editor: Thank you, Kristyn Winch, for always being that encouraging and critiquing editor I need. I'm glad you're willing to dive into the Romantasy world with me.

Our series had beautiful illustrations done by the amazing YukamiArt. Short review for those looking for an artist: She is absolutely one-of-a-kind. I've worked with her since 2021, and she's done an outstanding job. I will continue working with her on all my books. Thank you for your spectacular talent!

Thank you to my dreamy husband for providing me with a love that I can regale in countless stories that will always be swoon-worthy. You're my lighthouse, my pulse, my forever Jace.

And as always, thank you to the good Lord above for blessing me with the ability to write and the gift of creativity and imagination. All credit to Him.